Praise for
Those Fantastic Lives

"Best Southern Books of October 2021"
at Southern Review of Books
"Which Book Should You Read This Halloween?"
at Electric Literature

"*Those Fantastic Lives* is full of cinematic confections and concoctions. In deceptively buoyant prose that never sinks under the weight it carries, these stories are scary and funny and thrilling, sometimes all at the same time. I don't know if we should take this collection as a series of warnings, but being doomed has never been so enjoyable."

—Josh Denslow,
author of *Not Everyone is Special*

"Bradley Sides' debut collection, *Those Fantastic Lives*, is a treasure chest of dark wonder, one that brings to mind the best of Joe Hill and Ray Bradbury. It's perfect company for a stifling August night, or a rainy April morning, full of lovely places to get lost for a little while."

—Shaun Hamill,
author of *A Cosmology of Monsters*

"Urgent and energetic, frequently exuberant and always entertaining, this debut collection of stories is indeed just what we need right now: a fantastic array of fantastic fiction, in both quality and content."

—Fred Leebron,
author of *Six Figures* and *Welcome to Christiania*

"These exquisite but unsettling stories examine the fraught relationship between fear, love, and hope. Individually, they show Sides' skill at overlaying the real with the fantastic, contrasting innocence with malevolence. Together, they paint a picture of light driving out darkness, and love and hope—usually, but not always—overcoming fear."

—Jen McConnell,
author of *Welcome, Anybody*

"*Those Fantastic Lives* by Bradley Sides is a wonderfully curated collection that hones in on the concept of family as each story expands and converses with its neighbouring tales. Through tones that seem folkloric, Sides tells stories of grief and loss, the whirlwind nature of families, and of being an individual as a part of one, through a contemporary voice. Each story draws a connection in theme to others within this collection, but each presents these familiar themes and ideas through the lives of fantastic people and beings. […] In his stories of grief, loss, identity, and family, I am sure all readers can find themselves—and perhaps also their families—in the bits and pieces of each character and story."

—*Strange Horizons*

"One of the greatest things about Sides' writing is that he can make each story stand on its own while being stylistically different and still having a concise and cohesive writing style throughout. His writing is intricate enough to appeal to the masses and also to tickle the deepest literature genre fan. There is no doubt this collection of stories and his literary creations hereafter will be a successful venture, and in the end, Sides will ultimately be considered an important voice in the horror genre for a long time."

—Horror Obsessive

"Those Fantastic Lives is a book I, myself, couldn't and didn't want to put down. It's a Kelly Link-esque collection of stories that feeds but leaves you hungry for more; its beauty and strangeness create a brilliant cocktail that promises magic, wonder, and something straddling the in-between, and it delivers each in spades. Bradley Sides' work in this collection is incredibly detailed; the characters themselves feel like actors on a movie set rather than words dancing on a page — they breathe, they laugh, they cry."

—Southern Review of Books

"Bradley Sides uses magical realism to imbue everyday moments in his stories with a sense of eeriness and dread, but the true hauntings aren't the ghostly apparitions with sharp bared fangs, but the emotional ghosts that we're trying to outrun."

—Electric Literature

"Whether or not you consider yourself a dreamer — or a fan of magical realism — you will likely find something to believe in reading Sides' strange, beautiful stories. Many feel like fables, without relying on simple resolution or overarching metaphors. The author balances brisk plots with lively dialogue and flashes of poetic language."

—Nashville Scene

"Bradley Sides' new collection *Those Fantastic Lives* contains compelling pieces of fiction that use the speculative lens to terrify, delight, and aid us in pondering the true reality around us, and our relations to others within it. [...] The significance of emotional connection can be seen throughout the entire collection from start to finish. The losses, trials, fears, and triumphs that each of the many characters experience will resonate loud and clear in our hearts."

—Heavy Feather Review

"The collection goes beyond familiar narratives of the supernatural by asking *why* we are afraid of monsters and ghosts, and the things we cannot explain, illuminating the depths we as humans go to protect ourselves from what we are unable to comprehend."

—Fiction Writers Review

"Sides' new collection, *Those Fantastic Lives and Other Strange Stories,* is bold, unsettling, and always entertaining. Anyone seeking a quick trip into the unexpected will savor these tales."

—Cease, Cows

CROCODILE TEARS DIDN'T CAUSE THE FLOOD

Stories

Bradley Sides

MONTAG

A Montag Press Book
www.montagpress.com
Montag Press
777 Morton Street, Unit B
San Francisco CA 94129 USA

Montag Press, the burning book with the hatchet cover, the skewed word mark and the portrayal of the long-suffering fireman mascot are trademarks of Montag Press.

Printed & Digitally Originated in the United States of America
10 9 8 7 6 5 4 3 2 1

For Meredith, who gives my life
its magic…

CONTENTS

RAISING AGAIN

Both Eva and Girl, who was the human's small, amber-coated mix of a best friend, howled atop the roof of the only place they'd ever known as home. For the man who'd placed them there before the waves had taken him away. For the rains that had broken for the first time in a week to come back and take them, too. But it was already done. The man was long gone, and the water was receding.

As they looked to the sky, the moon performed a miracle. It returned.

It seemed braver upon its arrival. Bolder. Somehow more alive than before. So alive that it didn't stop when it filled to its brim with its splendid light. Soon, it spilled into the rest of the timid sky. Glowing. Burning. Like the sun.

There was such an abundance of brightness that Girl hid her eyes in the creases of Eva's soaked jeans. When she peeked again, she saw that the light wasn't only of the moon. The stars, which had been among the first to flee—after the birds—had found their way back, too.

But they seemed off. Weak. Confused. Their light diminished. Forgetting to float overhead. Instead, they fell.

Crashing and bouncing. And, then, they died.

Eva held Girl and tried her best to shelter the both of them as the curious fragments of the sky stormed upon and around them.

The celestial corpses dinged against Eva's arms and dug into Girl's back. Some smacked the tin on which the pair sat, and others landed onto the soggy ground and careened into the few oaks that remained rooted in the bleeding soil.

When the world went quiet, finally, Eva and Girl waited.

They watched above, below, and to each side, their bodies so close they couldn't tell which heart's rhythm belonged to whose body.

But nothing more came. Not in the immediate seconds that followed. Or in the minutes after that.

Eva got up and walked warily across the dented roof, and Girl trotted behind.

The human girl bent down and touched the just-gone stars. They blinked. Then went out again.

Girl nosed a few herself, becoming closer with the scent she had believed, only a few minutes gone, she and Eva would very well know.

Eva used her foot to sweep the surrounding stars into a pile, and then, she picked them up—one, and then another, collecting them and the ones Girl placed at her feet in the cradle of her small arms.

Slowly, these stars, sensing life, began to glow again.

Eva, with her arms stuffed full of stars, looked as if she were holding the moon itself.

Girl howled. She raised her head and called as far up into the sky as she could reach.

A prayer.

A thanksgiving.

Eva began howling herself, letting loose the fear and sadness she contained.

She threw her hands in the air, sending her bundle of burning stars back into the sky. And there they remained, floating higher and higher—all the way up, until they were back beside the moon.

In their place. In their home.

At the edge of the roof, Eva and Girl looked out into their world.

Above the graveyard of flickering stars, bright, beautifully glowing ones were shooting back up into the sky. To try again. Perhaps, believing that this time, it might be right.

Eva placed her hand softly on Girl's head, stroking the insides of her friend's ears and watching the beautiful show. Of light. Of reclaimed life. Of the world being put together again by those who remained.

Eva and Girl were so very tired, but they knew what they had to do.

Although it was still dark and hard to see, the spreading light from above would guide their way.

THE GUIDE TO KING GEORGE

Note: I hope these few words that I put together help guide you to many memorable years with the one who is—was, I guess—my best bud.
Be good to him!

—Ritchie

His Name:

The thing you'll be asked about the most is his name. It seems like just about all of the visitors at the amusement farm ask why the resident pond monster's name is King George. The truth is, I named him after my dad. His name was George.

Dad and I were tight. I guess most kids are close with their dads when they're seven, but me and my dad, we were different. We were best friends. Always hanging out. Playing. Gaming. You name it, we were having a good time doing it. Looking back, I know I shouldn't have done it, but I loved spending time with him so much that I started begging him to skip his naps before he had to go to work. I would talk him into building forts with me instead. Or get him to tell me ghost stories. Because of me, Dad fell asleep at the wheel on his way home from the factory one morning, ran off the road into the river, and got himself killed.

After he was gone, I wished all the time that he had been a king because I believed, for some reason, that kings lived forever. Stupid, I know, but that's what I thought as a little kid. If Dad had to die, I wanted to give my new best friend a chance at eternal life. Something that would keep me from losing him, too. So I named him King George.

But don't tell the farm's visitors all that. Just tell them we call him King George because he's the biggest pond monster in all the world. That'll do.

His Arrival, the Simple Answer:
"Where did he come from?" "How did he get here?" "Was he born in that pond?"

A form of one of these questions is what'll follow the whole name thing. It's up to you in how you choose to approach it.

If you want to pretend like I never existed, that's fine. Make up your own backstory for him. Maybe he was a tadpole in that very pond at which you'll be standing. Maybe he fell from the clouds. I don't know.

Or you can say that he came from the local pet store, Four-Legged Friends. Although hard to believe, that's actually the truth.

His Arrival, the Extended Answer:

After Dad died and Mom still didn't want to be in the picture, Gran and Gramps took me in.

My grandparents worried about me because they caught me crying in bed a lot. Like a whole lot. Their worrying got worse when they saw my notebook of drawings of me and Dad out in the river.

I heard Gran up at night talking to Gramps about me. He didn't say anything, as usual. But his agreement grunts hummed under Gran's words, so I wasn't surprised when she told me that I had to see a counselor.

When those visits didn't do much good, Gran and Gramps took me to group meetings with other kids who had recently-dead parents.

I went to those groups for a few months, but I missed Dad too much for them to help.

I just wanted to be by myself. I could remember him better when other people weren't talking to me or getting in the way.

Gran and Gramps eventually began to understand me a little, but they still thought I needed someone to talk to.

They more than thought it; they demanded it. "You are getting a friend, Ritchie," Gran started to say daily. "Oh yes, you are."

She and Gramps took me to the pet store on my birthday and told me to pick one out.

"Anything you want. A friend," Gran said, as the three of us walked through the automatic doors.

I didn't need to look for long. Honestly, he was right there. First aquarium. At the edge of the very front aisle. All alone in his glass enclosure. Swimming. He was actually swimming, like me and Dad used to do. A new kind of hybrid iguana-bullfrog species, staring at me—staring at me *and* swimming.

After we took him home, he stayed quiet the first couple of nights. It kind of freaked Gran and Gramps out that he didn't make any noise. I think they were afraid that he'd die, too, and that I wouldn't be able to handle it.

But soon he started talking—croaking. Anytime I went away, he started bellowing. Deep, gurgling bellowing. Honest to the gods, anytime I left his side, which was rare, he croaked and croaked.

Gran and Gramps thought it was great. They still stayed on me about the kids at school, but truthfully, I couldn't care less about the kids at school. Not then. Not ever. They were mean to me. Always had been, even before Dad died. "Freak" and "weirdo" were what they called me in the early days because they said I didn't talk enough, but after Dad died, they turned to whispering behind my back—or walking on the far side of the hallway, as far from me as they could get, like if they brushed up against me, they too might catch a case of sudden, accidental death. Honestly, Gran and Gramps could fuss to me about the kids at school all they wanted. At least I didn't hear them up at night anymore talking.

They could see the bond I had with King George. Even as a little, tiny thing, King George loved me, and I loved him, too.

When King George called, I answered.

I brought him whatever he needed. Food, mainly. At first it was flies, and then beetles. Next, he needed mice and worked his way up to chickens. Lots of chickens.

Obviously, he outgrew aquarium after aquarium, and, just a few weeks before my ninth birthday, there was nowhere else to put him other than out in the enormous pond behind the house.

I worried about him leaving the pond, since there wasn't a fence. Him crawling out of the water and going to the next pond. Or a lake. Or a river. Or *the* river. The one only a couple of miles down the road. The one Dad died in. But deep down, I believed he wouldn't ever choose to leave me.

When visitors ask me about how King George came to live in the pond, I say it's because of me.

I took him down to the pond, and *I* put him there in the water.

Makes me feel big like him to tell it. I bet you will too, if you want to give it a try.

Hours and Admission:

I'll include the boring but still necessary stuff about the farm in this section just to get it out of the way. We open on Memorial Day, and we close on Labor Day. Rain or shine, we are open every single day in this timeframe. This is only a summer gig. I hope Gran remembered to tell you. On weekdays, the first tour starts at nine o'clock sharp, and they continue at the top of each hour until the last one sets out from the barn at five. On weekends, we start an hour earlier and go an hour later. Twenty dollars per person. Kids under the age of five get in free. Veterans get a dollar discount. All guests stay on the trailer the entire time. You MUST strictly enforce that rule at the pond because King George doesn't really like a lot of people getting too close to him. I'm sure you read in the newspaper about the little kid he snapped at. It wasn't that big of a deal, but still. He is a pond monster, after all. Guests can take pictures. To be safe, we say no flash photography (just in case the light upsets King George), but it doesn't really matter. The flash has never bothered him before. The maximum number of guests per trailer is twelve. If more people are waiting, tell them they'll just have to wait until the next tour. People don't mind. They know what they're about to see.

The Amusement Farm:

I can't imagine anyone being interested in such a position as the one I've apparently left vacant without actually visiting the farm first, so I'm guessing you've been on one of the tours we offer.

As much of a basic familiarity as you might have, you still need a little history to get a better understanding of the place.

It'll come in handy. I promise.

The idea for the whole thing popped into Gran's head a few months after I'd had to put King George out in the pond. He was croaking louder and louder by the day because I was in school. And people around town were talking.

When me, Gran, and Gramps were selling corn and tomatoes at the local farmer's market one Saturday morning, which they always made me do with them because they thought it was good for my "social and emotional development," people kept on asking about the constant racket coming from our place. Gran and Gramps brushed off all of the nosiness. "It's just our grandson's pet. A harmless, sweet, huge thing. Honestly, he's like a great big teddy bear," Gran said.

But I couldn't take it anymore. I straight up lost it. "He's not a pet! He's my best friend!" I yelled. "He loves me, and he misses me. Badly!"

It shocked them both when I spoke up, but I'd had it.

After my outburst, those people raised their eyebrows all confused-like and walked away from our stand. They knew about my situation, so they tried to be nice to me.

But one lady who I didn't recognize didn't budge. She looked me dead in my eyes and said, "I'll pay you twenty dollars to go see this 'best friend' right now."

She was glaring at me, but she was actually making the proposal to Gran.

Gran started choking at the woman's offer.

Twenty dollars was a lot of money for us back then. My grandparents were living off their social security checks and what little money they made selling their fruits and vegetables. They hadn't planned on my arrival, my counseling sessions, or all the food King George was eating, so they were struggling. A woman offering free money wasn't something they could really turn down. So, after telling Gramps that was how it was going to be, Gran took the money, and I took the lady to see King George. To be fair, there wasn't a lot of seeing involved. I just walked her to the pond and pointed him out. With just a glance at him—seeing he actually existed, she took off screaming and crying. I didn't think much more about her really. Not until the next weekend, at least.

That very next Saturday morning, there she was back at our stand, and she had a couple of friends with her.

Gran tried to interest them in some apples, but they weren't in the mood. They just wanted to see King George.

Without missing a beat, Gran asked for another twenty dollars each, and I asked them to follow me out to the farm.

The woman didn't run this time. Neither did her friends. They stood there and watched my buddy carrying on in the pond. He wasn't all that big then, basically a grossly exaggerated gator. Imagine a dozen midnight blue industrial sized refrigerators wrapped together with a bungee cable. An oblong head at one end. A pointy tail at the other. Two wobbly baby legs and a set of bulging arms hanging off a saggy belly that, when full, tried its best to skirt against the pond's dirty bottom. That was him.

He showed out good, though. Belly flops, spinning, and splashing.

King George's first paying audience clapped when he went back into the water to rest, and they gave Gran an extra twenty-dollar bill. "That was awesome," the once-scared woman said.

At breakfast the next morning, Gran brought up the idea of turning King George into some kind of attraction. "What do you boys think about making some *real* money?" she asked.

She kept on talking about different possibilities with King George that by lunch she'd come up with not just a singular attraction, but the whole amusement farm idea.

When she told Gramps he could drive a tractor all day, hauling folks around from the barn to the pond, he snorted, which is more than you'll probably ever hear from him.

She told me I could train King George to perfect a few tricks. "Some like they do with the whales at that silly place in Florida," she said. "Splashy, showy stuff."

She would work the entrance and handle the accounts.

Right when it seemed like she was finished, she said she'd buy a badger and a couple of exotic birds to put up in different cages along the route to the pond. "For more variety," she said.

Three months later, the farm was open for business.

And that's how it began.

Trivia:

The farm's guests love trivia. It might be more that they just appreciate some kind of customer interaction. I know I'm not really entitled to criticize Gramps on this subject since I'm the way I am, but unless you count him grunting and tipping the sweaty end of his University of Tennessee ball cap as some kind of greeting, he doesn't even acknowledge our guests. Ever.

King George gets off on their excitement. You can tell when he's getting amped because he starts shaking really badly. It's almost like he's doing some kind of shoulder shimmy without having the actual shoulders to do the shimmy. Little waves start forming around his head and he just gets to bobbing away. So, to make him happy, I usually offer the guests a little something. I throw out a question that I know will stump them.

I ask them if they know the amusement farm's actual name.

You should keep this question going.

I promise. The guests eat it up.

Do you know the answer? I'm sure you don't. Nobody ever does. Everybody thinks it's just called "The Amusement Farm." Even on the ads that Gran put in the paper, "The Amusement Farm." On the radio, back when Gran paid for advertisement there, "The Amusement Farm."

Anyhow, the farm's named *George's*. It's actually named after Dad and not the pond monster everybody is so eager to see. I know because Gran let me name it.

There's even a sign out front displaying a cartoon version of me and Dad acting like we are scared of a monster bubbling beneath the surface of the pond beside us. Dad's arm is wrapped around my shoulders, and I'm beside him real tight. Tree branches cover most of the sign now, so you probably didn't know it was there. But it is. I think about it a lot.

The Daily Schedule During Season:
A good bulleted list is easy on the eyes, so I'll help you out here:

- Be at Gran and Gramp's house no later than 6:00 a.m.
- Grab the bucket outside the back door. I never bothered with washing it but once a week, but you'll have to determine what you can handle on your own. It sure gets to stinking.
- Take the bucket and head out to Gramps' barn.
- Open the big doors and reach your hand over to the right.
- You'll find a switch. Flip it on, and go to the freezer, which is pretty much right under the light switch.
- Open the freezer and fill the bucket with as many dead chickens as you can. Gramps buys these in bulk from somebody, so there'll never be any problems with not having enough.
- Close the lid.

- Turn off the light.

- Shut the door.

- Walk down the dirt path to the pond. The sun won't be up yet, so enjoy the darkness. I've always found it comforting.

- Be out on the northern bank of the pond before the sun rises. Like clockwork, King George will pop his head up from the water when the sun peeks over the trees. That'll be your cue.

- Take the chicken carcasses and toss them out into the water. Once you get to know him better, he might eat out of your hands. He always did for me. He might even let you pet him, but that'll probably take some time.

- Talk to him. Tell him how important he is to you. How he's your best friend. How you don't know what you'd do without him. Sing to him maybe. He enjoys a good song. Mostly lullabies. Turn on the fog machine. The plug is over by the big oak on the eastern side. While this little addition is more for the upcoming audience, I think King George gets a kick out of it. He's certainly never complained. Hang out with him until you hear the first tour group coming. (Don't forget that you have extra time during the week, but you probably won't notice he's such good company.) There's no way to miss the tractor. It's about forty years old and smokes like crazy. During your first few days, you'll probably think a fire has struck the barn.

- Once you see the trailer, it's time to get King George moving. The guests get excited when they see him for the first time. They start to standing and clapping—and cheering, too, like they are at one of those rivalry football games that Gramps likes to watch on the television. Snap your fingers three times and point toward the sun. King George will fly out of the water. When he's up there, fall down on the dirt. Fast. Basically, collapse. He'll come down and do a huge belly flop. Most of the water will shoot straight up, but a few drops will hit the audience. A free souvenir, they think, so they never mind. Somehow almost all of the water makes its way back into the pond. Even if it doesn't, it's nothing to worry about. The rain is reliable around here.

- Gramps will pull the trailer there beside you. People will be standing and howling. Do it all again. Have King George raise up, fly, and splash back down right in front of the guests.

- Once he settles back into the water, start nodding your head kind of slowly and make a circular movement with your fist closed. King George will start making laps, with his head bobbing in and out of the water. His speed will match yours, so get progressively faster. You'll know when it's enough by the crowd's reaction. The trailer will be rocking. Allow him to rest for a couple of minutes. Make sure to give him this time. That episode when he snapped at the stupid little kid was because I didn't. As

King George recoups, interact with the farm's visitors. The easiest way to do this is to ask the trivia question. Allow them to ask a question or two. I've already supplied you with those answers above.

- Step away and tell them to make sure to get their cameras ready. That you'll give them one more belly flop.

- Wait until they've stopped cheering and have their phones out.

- Run back down to the bank and point your finger upward, this time stretching as far as you can to the sky. Like you yourself might fly off the ground. King George will give it all he has if you do. Then, collapse. When King George makes his big splash, Gramps will get the trailer going on its way.

- Have King George do another few laps as the trailer disappears back down the path from which it came.

- Sit down on the bank and relax. You might need some cold compresses for those first few days until your body gets used to all the falling. Talk to King George until the next group comes. Then, do it all over again.

- Repeat this same process until your shift is done.

- Once the day is over, hang out with King George for as long as you want. I usually stay until close to midnight. I tell him about Dad and all the fun we used to have. How I miss him.

- Head back to the barn and put everything where it goes. Doing so will make the next morning easier.

Dress Code:

I always wear my official *unofficial* uniform. If we are the same size, I'm sure Gran and Gramps will let you have my things. If my clothes don't fit you, buy the following items: rubber mud boots, a long sleeve shirt to keep the sun off of you, jeans, and a wide-brim straw hat.

Breaks and Lunch:

There are no scheduled breaks or lunches. Figure that part out on your own. Gramps brings me water sometimes, but honestly, I get so carried away on most days that I don't think about eating.

The Daily Schedule During Off-Season:

You have more flexibility in the off-season. I, for example, like to sleep out on the banks beside him most nights and not even bother with going to my room since I have to leave him for school for a big chunk of the day. Well, when I actually go to school. I skip most of the time and tell Gran and Gramps my stomach hurts. My teachers know about my past, so they don't ever argue. I just hang out with King George all day every day. He doesn't seem to mind, and I know I am happy watching him. Being with him.

Safety:

I haven't told you this quite yet, but a few weeks ago, King George started seeming kind of off. He wasn't coming as close to me or splashing as much. It was like he was distracted or sad or something. So, I started swimming with him.

While I'm out there, I jump on him. I howl and splash the dirty algae water. We play. I thought it would cheer him up, and it was fun, but I can tell there's something missing between us. I think it's that I'm not as special to him anymore. I mean, now he has the farm's guests clapping for him all the time. All the camera flashes. The cheers.

Nowadays, when he's playing with me, he doesn't fully let loose. He doesn't roar. He doesn't shimmy. Nothing like that at all.

Gran tells me I need to stop getting in the pond with King George. That I'm risking my life and the farm's life, too. To make her feel better, I told her I'd write this manual for whomever might replace me. She fussed, but she agreed it was best.

She doesn't know why, of all things, I swim with King George to try to cheer him up, but I'll tell you.

On the weekend before Dad's accident, we were swimming at a random creek somewhere off a little road in the middle of nowhere. I was on his back, and we were both squealing and laughing and smiling and just absolutely consumed with love. I thought I was on top of the world. It's my favorite memory. Of my whole entire life, that very one is it.

Although I know what it'll cost me, I owe it to my best bud to keep trying to recreate that feeling of love for him.

And after I fail, I need you to succeed. King George deserves as much.

OUR PATCHES

Back on one of the nights in what had to be our second week—after the crying softened and the angry, delusional threats of escape went away—the generator went down. In the darkness, we shuffled to our cots to rest. We no longer looked through the cut tempered glass at the sizzle of ash falling upon the land. We already knew all we would need to know. Janis, our eldest, suggested, in the silence, the idea for individual patches. "For a quilt," she explained. She said she had made them her entire life. So, too, had her mother, and her mother's mother. "Someone, one day, needs to know that each of us lived—that *we* lived."

As she finished her words, the familiar hum that we had taken for granted started again, and the lights returned. This was the only sign we needed.

We leapt from our hard beds, old and young alike, and took to our extra clothes in the bags we had kept up in our closets for years, ready for escape. We grabbed our white sheets and pillowcases, too. And the soft blue blankets upon our cots.

We ripped them, like we were animals.

Hungry.

Lustful.

We tore them in such a way that if the ash would have taken a break from its destruction, it might have been equally impressed by the storm brewing below it. It might have even taken a break and watched. Learned something with the way we quickly demonstrated our purpose.

We asked Janis to teach us, pushing our cots against the wall and joining her on the cold floor. "Gather a memory. A moment," she told us. "Close your eyes and see what comes."

And when we opened our eyes, after finding that part of ourselves we wanted to go on for forever, we turned to watch her hands.

The way she cut with her scissors.

Held her thread.

Moved her thimble.

Worked her needle.

There, on the floor, we began our patches. Talking and laughing as we trimmed and measured, sharing our chosen stories that would outlast us. About the creek in which one of us trapped minnows in Mason jars. The picnic table where another ate the sour rinds of yellow-meated watermelon. The rainstorm two of us danced in. And even, we admitted with acceptance, the ash storm that was as big a part of our lives as anything else.

The gases that seep through the door have slowed us, but, still, we stitch. With as much purpose and hope as we can.

We are nearly finished. We are. We are.

TO TAKE, TO LEAVE

(**1**) You were lonely, so you took in the boy. No matter how much you try to justify your role in this whole thing by how much you love him, the apocalypse is your fault.

Speaking of the apocalypse, death is coming, and it's coming at you fast—so fast that you won't escape it if you don't do something. Soon. You better do that something soon.

There's a lake of fire burning through Ms. Jackson's brand-new cut and loop carpet just across the way, and no matter how much baking soda or salt the old woman tosses at those wet, angry flames, they are only spreading—*quickly*.

Wooden planks, concrete bricks, and bird carcasses are cascading from overhead. Outside, for now.

You know this because you look out your living room window and see your yard. Well, not really so much your *yard*, but the multiple layers of death and destruction that continue to pile on top of it.

You think of Alex and Caleb, the stoner kids who mow your lawn. You, like their own parents, are mad at them. You want this to be their fault. You want this to be anyone else's fault.

But it's not. It's yours.

A creaking sound above your head steals your attention, and it's now that you realize you should've acted on one of those postcard advertisements the roofing company's been leaving in your mailbox for the past two springs.

Oh, and there's a smell that's about to hit you. Just wait. It's a bad, bad smell.

-If you want to give up, stop here. Death certainly won't be long.

-If you want to try to fight, proceed to (2).

(2) You should know more about that smell. It's gas. There's a leak in the den. It's firing up, too.

Firing. Haha.

The odor hits you, and you imagine the coming explosion. Then you don't. You don't really imagine a lot. You actually start to feel kind of woozy.

Despite the gas, you close your eyes and take a deep breath.

You choke. You choke some more. Then you calm down, surprisingly.

You count to ten. Sort of. You forget six, seven, nine, and ten. It doesn't matter.

Things start to feel pretty good. Great even.

-If you've changed your mind and want to embrace this "great" feeling, stop here.

-If you are sure about forging ahead, proceed to (3).

(3) You yell a word. Two words. "Nine!" "Ten!"

Maybe you didn't forget.

Regardless, you persevere.

You tell yourself to get a grip. Literally. "Get a grip," you whisper.

You hear yourself, too. The quiet echo of your voice. It startles you because it's now that you realize you are, of all things, in this room by yourself.

Alone.

The reason for the current apocalypse can be traced back to you not wanting to be alone. You shouldn't be in this state now, especially with the end of the world coming.

You need to find him.

You need to find your son. Your "little man."

You scan the room just to be sure he isn't hiding, but you don't see him.

You walk to the hallway, and he's there. In plain sight.

He's on the wooden stairs. Waiting.

He's holding your battery-powered radio in his small, gloved hands.

Your spacesuit-wearing son is sitting, properly helmeted in his pure white suit, as always, in the comfort of his swirling indigo breaths of fire.

He seems so peaceful, maybe eager.

You want to talk to your son. Tell him it's okay. Tell him you forgive him. Tell him you love him no matter what. But you can't because something else captivates you. It's a voice, and it trembles over the radio's broken speakers. You know it, although you can't place exactly how.

"World exploding," the voice says, choking back tears. "Lava flowing." "Islands sinking," it says.

At this moment, you look to your son. You meet his eyes so you are reminded why allowing this to happen is okay. As soon as you meet his gaze, though, your roof collapses. It collapses on you.

❧⊙❧

A haunting buzz of static takes over the airways, takes over your now burnt-orange, crushed shell of a house. What's left of it.

You, through the rubble, run to your son.

No, you don't really *run*. You jump. You climb. You go to him.

He's still on the stairs. Untouched, unmoved. Miraculously, you think, but you realize quickly this is no miracle. No, no. This is prophecy.

You reach for him. You grasp him. You don't stop until you fully embrace him. Through a slick material you've never recognized, behind a glass that keeps you from ever touching his face.

Although you don't know how exactly to say it, you want to talk to him. You want to tell him you don't care. That it has all been worth it. That he has.

But you don't. Instead, he speaks. He knows the perfect words.

"I will save you," he tells you. You struggle to hear him because the helmet blocks his words, but you still make it out. You do because you want to. Or need to. No, you do because you have to. "I've always told you so. Since you saved me. We are going to be okay."

-If you want a second chance at preventing the apocalypse, proceed to (4).
-If you believe your son, skip to (7).

(4) It's three years earlier and, like every day since your parents abandoned you for their Caribbean Island condo a decade ago, you are alone.

You are also something else, strangely. You are hopeful.

For the first time in four days, you are out of your bed and looking out your window.

You are—yes—hopeful, wishing for something. Anything, really. *Anyone.*

This is your lucky day because you get your wish.

It comes first as a squirrel. It's drinking water out of the dirty, chipped birdbath you've been intending to clean. The one you swore to your mother you'd take care of when she and your father left you. But you disregard the filth. You smile. You even sort of laugh.

You stay at the window, and a family of bumblebees fly by, eventually brushing against the tops of yellow flowering weeds that suffocate your sidewalk.

Being up is going well for you—so well that you want to watch the sunset.

You never do this. Never. You haven't been outside in over a week. Not since you went to the Stock 'N Save on that Thursday nine days ago and broke the last hundred-dollar bill your parents left you.

Today, though, you watch. For a long time, you do.

You finally turn away from the tangerine glow behind Ms. Jackson's bungalow just when it's almost gone, and you glance at your mailbox and, then, at the end of your driveway. Your wandering vision-trip continues down your sidewalk and to the very glass in front of you.

You sigh and step away from the window.

You've only taken a handful of steps when something tells you to go back.

You have nothing else to do, and today has been surprisingly okay. So you listen, and you go.

You lean so closely to the glass that the tip of your nose sweats, and the window fogs. You see something. In your driveway. Something small. Something burning.

You stare at the light, at the purple, smokey sparks of flame that burn at the end of your driveway, and your heart skips a beat. A couple of beats.

You need to go out. You need to go out now.

You look for your shoes, but you don't know where they are. You decide you don't care.

-If you've decided all this adrenaline is too much, go on back to bed. Your journey ends here.
-If you can't pass up this opportunity, proceed to (5).

(5) You step out of your front door with no shoes on, and you sprint down your sidewalk. But you only make it a few steps before you cut your foot on a jagged, stray pebble from your chipped cement path.

You leap to the grass, and you brush off the sole of your foot. There's blood, but you rub it against your shirt. It's a white t-shirt, but you don't care.

You run atop the clover and weeds all the way to the edge of your driveway. All the way to the indigo flames.

When you look down, you can't believe what you see. It's the very thing you used to pray for. The thing your parents used to say you needed. The thing your former coworkers suggested over and over again. The thing that they all said would heal you, would save you.

You don't even have to see its face to know what it is. You already know, and you know for certain.

On the ground is a child.

Your child, you already think.

It has fallen. You know this. You know it. Something inside you knows it.

The child is facedown, but it's breathing. It's definitely breathing. Cloudy, purple breaths that time perfectly with the rise and fall of the child's back puff slowly down a tube that travels into a translucent purifier attached to the—*your*—little one's back.

You roll your child over, and you see its face. His face.

The smoke trapped inside his helmet makes it hard to see his eyes, but you finally glimpse them—his sparkling, ocean-like eyes—when he exhales deeply.

You put your hands to his helmet. To take it off. To tell him he will be okay. To tell him you will save him. But his hands meet yours just before you touch it, and he shakes his head.

You don't even feel the heat radiating from the helmet. You don't care. All you can think about is him. His presence. His arrival.

A raindrop sizzles as it falls onto the boy's helmet. Then another. And, then, another. You look up and see storm clouds. They are coming.

-If you leave the child outside, your journey ends here. You go back inside and crawl into bed. The day, you decide, has been too long already, and you've stepped way too far out of your comfort zone.
-If you take the child inside, proceed to (6).

(6) When you carry him through your door, you place him on your couch. Your arms brush against his searing helmet as you let him go. You don't scream. You don't say anything at all. Instead, you run to your refrigerator and stick your red, burning arms inside your ice maker.

You want to cry, but not from the pain.

You go back to the boy, this time with two towels. You fold them and place them under his head.

You do this for his comfort and not for your couch's protection, although you realize you've done both.

"I'm sorry," he says.

Whether his apology is for the inconvenience, your burnt arms, or your toasted couch cushions, you don't know. Or care.

"It's okay," you say.

You take his hand, and you hold it. These are the first hands you've held in years.

When he falls asleep, you don't let go. You don't do anything all night except stare at your boy. You don't go outside and look for parents—or spaceships, or fire-breathing kin, or anything or anyone else that might belong to him.

You don't do this because you claim him as your own. Immediately, you do.

After a few days, he sits up, and he thanks you. He thanks you for helping him. For being good to him.

He says, "You are going to be okay. I will save you."

You don't ask from what. You never do.

You just believe him. You believe him because he already has.

-If you want to prevent the apocalypse, it's not too late. Head back to (4).
-If you love your son and just want to be with him at the world's end, proceed to (7).

(7) Your son stands and reaches for your hand.

-If you take it, proceed to (8).
-If you—no, no—you've already made your choice. You take your boy's hand. Proceed to (8).

(8) You follow him as he makes his way from the still-standing staircase and leads you out of the smoldering house. You go with him all the way out into your yard. You tell him it's not safe. You tell him to be careful. You tell him you should both go back inside. Or what's left of inside.

But he doesn't listen. He, with his hand tucked into yours, continues on, and you never resist. You go right with him. Perfectly in sync.

You don't understand what he's doing. Truthfully you don't. Not as he takes you to a clear spot in your backyard that's somehow still alive and beautiful. Not even when you are standing, perfectly safe, under a tree. Your oak tree. The only tree in your entire neighborhood still remaining. The only tree in the whole world still remaining.

You still don't understand as the shouting and crying and sirens blare around you. As the sound of hissing tears falling onto the decaying world sizzle.

You still don't understand when you look into the sky and see how the clouds have already gone elsewhere.

It's not until your boy speaks that you finally start to get it. "You might not want to watch this," he says, as he takes off his helmet. Your boy, the boy you saved and loved after he crashed on his quest to end the world, gulps in one giant breath. The longest breath you've ever witnessed.

When he opens his mouth, he releases the fire.

You really, really get it when he releases the fire. When the wild flames smother everything surrounding you. When you imagine the disintegration of Ms. Jackson and Alex and Caleb and your old coworkers and your parents and the beautiful beach they live on. When he holds you in his arms and you blast off, with him, happily, into the sky.

FESTIVAL OF KITES

Boxes arrive suspended from nylon parachutes sometime overnight as the future participants rest, work, and play. At daybreak, on this grand holiday, the lids are opened, the materials ceremoniously unpacked. Oohs and aahs stir for rolls of emerald silk, cherry dowels, scissors, tape, glue, string, and gleaming white ribbon. Then, slowly, meticulously, using most of the day's best light, lost in both conversation and silence, humankind the world over constructs kites. Millions upon millions of beautiful kites. The anxious look for clues, going outside as the time approaches, their creations in hand, seeing if the wind might nip or if it might at least twirl the sprig of extra string from the bridling point. But, no. They, like the resolved, must wait until sunset, which nears the horizon. And as it approaches—closer, closer—the participants line their lawns and streets and fields, for there is no hiding, no safety to be found in isolated cabins or overgrown jungles. Not in cloud-flirting chateaus either. They all come. They must, and they must come with their kites. As the sun lowers and lowers, and the soft orange shadows slip into paling, dying blues, the participants suit up, draping their kites over their backs. Sliding their arms through and over the wooden rods. Parents instruct their children to follow their lead. The old, those in beds and chairs, ask, plead with waiting neighbors and tired family members. To help. To please, help. They all wait. There are no announcements for when the Festival will begin. No songs or speeches. The wind simply comes, its initial breeze loving—comforting, even—sweeping in so softly, so delicately, as if the ceremony is but a dream that lifts the yearly chosen. Mostly the old and sick, but with surprises. There is a precious moment to say goodbye. To touch. To kiss. To temporarily hold. To say and repeat those three words they all know so well, and have silently rehearsed all day—and week and month and year—as the wind comes stronger and stronger again. Those in flight lose their faces as they rise. They become only kites. Dozens, hundreds, thousands, as they lift higher and higher into the clouds. Those below, still wearing their wings, wave goodbye even as the moon settles in for a cool night's stay. They wonder—fear, dream—when it will be their turn to take to the sky. To fly.

THE BROWNE
TRANSCRIPT

(DOOR SLAMS AGAINST FRAME)

Jonathan Browne: Come on, man! I brought my jar.

Detective Murphy: My apologies. Been telling maintenance to tighten the plate for months. Busy, I guess.

Jonathan Browne: *(HUFF)*

Detective Murphy: Jonathan Browne?

Jonathan Browne: Technically, I guess.

Detective Murphy: Technically?

Jonathan Browne: Birth certificate name is Jonathan Elijah Browne. Everybody calls me Eli. Have since I was a boy.

Detective Murphy: Okay. I'll stick with Mr. Browne if it's the same with you.

Jonathan Browne: Doesn't matter what you call me.

Detective Murphy: I'm Detective Thomas Murphy. Do you understand why you're here, Mr. Browne?

Jonathan Browne: I suppose.

Detective Murphy: It's not really an "I suppose" kind of question. Do you or do you not?

Jonathan Browne: I brought myself down here, didn't I?

(*CHAIR SCRAPES AGAINST FLOOR AND CUSHION EXHALES*)

Detective Murphy: (*GRUNT*)

(*PAUSE*)

Detective Murphy: You know you may ask for an attorney at any point in the questioning if you feel as if you need one?

Jonathan Browne: I don't.

Detective Murphy: If you change—

Jonathan Browne: I won't change my mind.

Detective Murphy: Okay. Do you need anything before we get started? Water? Coffee?

Jonathan Browne: Other than for people to start listening to me, no.

Detective Murphy: I don't think I can help you much with that.

Jonathan Browne: Guess not.

Detective Murphy: Would you like it if I could?

Jonathan Browne: It would certainly be for the best for most everybody. Are you a man of faith?

Detective Murphy: I don't see why that matters, Mr. Browne.

(*PAUSE*)

Jonathan Browne: Are you?

Detective Murphy: In what?

Jonathan Browne: Whatever you want. Whoever.

Detective Murphy: I'd say so. Yes.

Jonathan Browne: Good.

(*PAUSE*)

Detective Murphy: I see.

Jonathan Browne: Can we begin?

Detective Murphy: So that's them, huh?

Jonathan Browne: Why else would I carry a glass jar around?

Detective Murphy: The moths don't seem very special to me.

(*GLASS SCRAPES AGAINST TABLE*)

Jonathan Browne: I don't think something has to look special for it to be special, man of faith.

Detective Murphy: (*GRUNT*) They look old. All three of them. Got tattered wings and something on them. Dust? Dirt?

(*PAUSE*)

Detective Murphy: What is that you've gotten in there with them? A rotten apple or something?

Jonathan Browne: Can we begin?

Detective Murphy: I guess we better.

(*GLASS SCRAPES AGAINST TABLE*)

Detective Murphy: (*GRUNT*) Where were you last night, the night of August 17th, Mr. Browne?

Jonathan Browne: Same place I am every night.

Detective Murphy: Mr. Browne, your tone. I'd suggest you rethink—

Jonathan Browne: Fine. I'm just a little agitated.

Detective Murphy: I understand. A man in your situation with your family gone—

Jonathan Browne: They are not gone. I'm agitated because no one will listen to me.

Detective Murphy: Mr. Browne, I'm listening, so let's try again. Where were you on the night of August 17th?

Jonathan Browne: Same place I am every night. At home.

Detective Murphy: At home? And what were you doing at home?

Jonathan Browne: Sitting in my rocker staring at the TV, watching Billygoat Lewis defend his title from that new kid.

Detective Murphy: I see—

Jonathan Browne: Flex Money.

Detective Murphy: (*GRUNT*)

Jonathan Browne: Flex Money is the new kid. Was supposed to be the next big thing in the wrestling world. That's what everybody wants at least, but I hate him. Cocky and wears too much lipstick. Can't stand those orange trunks he wears either. Too pretty. Looks like a movie star instead of a wrestler.

Detective Murphy: Back to the question. What were you doing other than watching TV? Who were you with, Mr. Browne?

Jonathan Browne: With?

Detective Murphy: At home. Who were you with at home?

Jonathan Browne: Myself mainly.

Detective Murphy: Mainly?

Jonathan Browne: I was by myself in the living room. My family doesn't much care for wrestling.

Detective Murphy: Oh.

Jonathan Browne: They say it's a "bunch of fake crap."

Detective Murphy: (*UNINTELLIGIBLE*)

Jonathan Browne: They were home, though. Back in their own rooms, on their stupid little phones, I'm sure. Like always. Tweetering and all that. You know, nothing involving "fake crap."

Detective Murphy: Go on.

Jonathan Browne: With what?

Detective Murphy: Who were you with?

Jonathan Browne: My family. My wife, daughter, and son. I named him after Billygoat. He doesn't like me to tell that, but it's the truth. I asked his mama if we had a boy if—

Detective Murphy: Mr. Browne, you do realize your entire family is missing, correct? And you are a suspect—

Jonathan Browne: They aren't missing. I'm looking right at them.

Detective Murphy: You are looking at a jar of moths! (*CLEARS THROAT*)

(*PAUSE*)

Detective Murphy: You are looking at a jar of moths, Mr. Browne, and you are telling me about a wrestler you seem to be a fan of. I want to know where your family is, and I want to know if you are the one who can point me in the direction of their location.

Jonathan Browne: I was asked to come down here, and it's because of the free audience to which I can tell the truth—even if that audience is only one person— that I'm here. Now, my family is fine, and they'll still be doing fine once the fires come.

Detective Murphy: So, a fire's coming now?

Jonathan Browne: Not *now* now. But soon.

Detective Murphy: What?

Jonathan Browne: A fire is not coming now. It's coming at the rise of the morning two days from now.

Detective Murphy: So, a fire is coming? And it's coming not tomorrow morning, but the next morning?

Jonathan Browne: Yep.

Detective Murphy: You are causing me a lot of frustration right now, Mr. Browne.

Jonathan Browne: It's not me you should be frustrated by. I'm trying to help save the ones we can. There's going to be a lot of folks go "missing" tonight. Tomorrow's the full moon. The big one.

(*HAND SLAPS TABLE*)

Jonathan Browne: (*UNINTELLIGIBLE*) You break my jar, and I'm going to be answering some different questions, Detective Murphy, and I'm afraid you won't be the one doing the asking.

Detective Murphy: Are you threatening me, Mr. Browne?

Jonathan Browne: Don't break my jar.

Detective Murphy: Back to last night.

Jonathan Browne: Huh?

Detective Murphy: Back. To. Last. Night. Mr. Browne, you are just blabbing a lot of mumbo jumbo. Back to last night.

Jonathan Browne: What about it?

Detective Murphy: You were watching wrestling at your home. Your family members were in their own respective rooms. What else?

Jonathan Browne: There's not much else to say. Not really. I knew it was coming. Been having the dream for the past week. A dream as real as life. I just didn't know exactly when the whole moth thing was happening. I mean, I knew it would be soon because the 20th is it for a lot of us. The morning of the 20th, like I said.

Detective Murphy: But what else did you do that night, Mr. Browne?

Jonathan Browne: I tried to spend all the time I could with them—all of them. Even called out of my mail route all week, but my family—they didn't believe a word I said. Doubters. (*UNINTELLIGIBLE*)

Detective Murphy: I'm sorry, but what?

Jonathan Browne: Look. It's pretty simple. I watched Billy-goat's interview after the match, and as soon as it was over, I turned off the TV and went to tell my kids goodnight. Bill first because he's not usually too difficult. He's still young, you know? World hasn't gotten to him yet. Not too bad at least.

Detective Murphy: Go on.

Jonathan Browne: I'm trying to.

Detective Murphy: (*UNINTELLIGIBLE*)

Jonathan Browne: I opened his bedroom door, and everything was in place just like he was in there. Overhead light was off, but the fan was going. Phone on his pillow. Some kind of racket coming from his headphones. Weird, head-banging kind of music. I don't know where he got that taste from. Sure wasn't me. Loud. Screamo mess—

Detective Murphy: I don't care about the music.

(*PAUSE*)

Jonathan Browne: The indention was still there…

Detective Murphy: What?

(*PAUSE*)

Jonathan Browne: It must've just happened. I could see where his head had been on his pillow. Even touched the little, shallow hole there, and it was warm. The whole room was warm, but I still got chills when I saw that pillow.

Detective Murphy: So you're telling me your son vanished while in his room? Was there any sign of an intruder or was anything—

Jonathan Browne: He didn't vanish. He transformed.

Detective Murphy: Transformed?

Jonathan Browne: Yes, he transformed into a moth.

Detective Murphy: Were you upset about anything going on at home or at work? Anything your son might've said to you? Your daughter? Wife? A boss?

Jonathan Browne: I didn't hurt my family. I'm saving them.

Detective Murphy: Your moth family?

Jonathan Browne: Yes.

(*PAUSE*)

Jonathan Browne: You shall take them and shall protect them until it is time for them to go safely on home. You shall take them and shall protect them until it is time for them to go safely on home. You shall take them and shall protect them until it is time for them to go safely—

Detective Murphy: Stop! Stop! What are you talking about?

Jonathan Browne: The dream. It's the words.

Detective Murphy: That's what your dream told you over and over again, and you have concocted a whole story about moth transformations and a burning world?

Jonathan Browne: I see the other stuff. It's clear. I'm telling you.

(*PAUSE*)

Jonathan Browne: Are you a man of faith, Detective Murphy?

Detective Murphy: What?

Jonathan Browne: Are you a man of faith?

Detective Murphy: You've already asked me that. Yes. Yes, I am.

Jonathan Browne: Good. So you believe?

Detective Murphy: In what?

Jonathan Browne: In whatever? In—

(*HAND SLAPS TABLE*)

Jonathan Browne: My jar, Detective Murphy.

Detective Murphy: Back to the night! Back to last night!

(*PAUSE*)

Detective Murphy: Where, Mr. Browne, did you find this moth son of yours after Bill allegedly vanished from his bedroom?

Jonathan Browne: He didn't vanish from his bedroom. He was still there.

Detective Murphy: Where?

Jonathan Browne: He was fluttering against his lamp. Light was on, and he was there, wings flapping. He knows to go to the light. It's built into them. These moths. They know. That's why they are becoming moths.

Detective Murphy: So, after you turned off your wrestling program, you went into your son's room, and he, as a moth, was flapping against a lightbulb?

Jonathan Browne: Yes.

Detective Murphy: This is ridiculous. (*CHAIR SCRAPES AGAINST FLOOR*)

(*PAUSE*)

Detective Murphy: What did you do once you saw him?

Jonathan Browne: I had a jar ready, with holes poked in the lid. Even had a piece of a nectarine in the bottom. Nectarine, not an apple. A tiny bit of honeysuckle. A couple of sticks for him—them—to rest on.

Detective Murphy: (*UNINTELLIGIBLE*)

Jonathan Browne: I softly pinched the edge of his wings, and I put him in the jar. Screwed on the lid. Went to catch my daughter and wife.

Detective Murphy: And they were moths, too, I guess?

Jonathan Browne: Yep.

Detective Murphy: In their rooms? Fluttering around?

Jonathan Browne: Yep. Daughter was perched on one of those little strings that drops down from her overhead light. Don't know what you call those things. Wife was tapping against the window above our bed. Trying, already, to get on out of here. Headed toward the moon.

Detective Murphy: Mr. Browne, was there anything going on at home that had you upset? Was your family upset? Your kids fighting with you? Your wife say something? Do something? Anything—

Jonathan Browne: I didn't hurt my family.

Detective Murphy: Do you have reason to believe someone else could've been upset with your family?

Jonathan Browne: No. No one is upset with my family, and no one has hurt my family.

Detective Murphy: This is insane.

Jonathan Browne: You've made that opinion very clear.

Detective Murphy: Well, it is.

Jonathan Browne: In the dream, they are safe. I'm telling you. They are. I can see them flying, escaping. Landing on the moon's surface. Starting over in a better place.

(*PAUSE*)

Detective Murphy: As humans or moths?

Jonathan Browne: Both and neither.

Detective Murphy: What?

Jonathan Browne: It's hard to explain. I don't know. I can just see their eyes. They are happy. They just are. Being better than we are now.

Detective Murphy: What does that even mean, Mr. Browne?

Jonathan Browne: I think it's a punishment.

Detective Murphy: What is?

Jonathan Browne: This.

Detective Murphy: For what?

Jonathan Browne: Us.

Detective Murphy: So, you are a bad man?

Jonathan Browne: Not particularly. No.

Detective Murphy: Then why aren't you one of these moths? Escaping and going on to an alleged better place. Partaking in all the coming lollipops and rainbows.

Jonathan Browne: Not for me to say.

Detective Murphy: What?

Jonathan Browne: It's not for me to say why I'm not one of the chosen. My role is to get the others to safety, and I'm trying the best I can to do so.

(*PAUSE*)

Jonathan Browne: Always thought of myself as a faithful man. Trying to prove it. Live it, I guess you could say.

Detective Murphy: Makes two of us, then, right?

Jonathan Browne: We'll see.

(*PAUSE*)

Detective Murphy: Back to last night, Mr. Browne. So, you caught your family of moths, and you did what?

Jonathan Browne: I put them on my nightstand, and I went to sleep.

Detective Murphy: Let me get this straight. You were able to sleep after your family allegedly transformed into moths?

Jonathan Browne: Yes. Quite peacefully actually.

(*PAUSE*)

Jonathan Browne: The dream came again, like I knew it would.

(*PAUSE*)

Jonathan Browne: I've been writing to the paper, Detective Murphy. Been making videos. Been shouting about it at the dollar store. The bank. Cheapies when I go to get milk. Telling everyone to get ready. Those of us left behind will have to keep the others safe. It'll be up to us to make sure that our loved ones get to their new home.

Detective Murphy: I see.

Jonathan Browne: You shall take them and shall protect them until it is time for them to go safely on home.

Detective Murphy: Yes, yes. You've said that. How long have you been writing to the paper? Making the videos and carrying on?

Jonathan Browne: Since I woke up from my first dream. About a week ago, like I said. I'm sure people have called the station. They won't listen to what I'm trying to tell them.

Detective Murphy: I wonder why?

Jonathan Browne: Huh?

Detective Murphy: You've been planning this then?

Jonathan Browne: No, I wouldn't say "planning."

Detective Murphy: Several of your neighbors have been very concerned, Mr. Browne. You know that, correct?

Jonathan Browne: I can't say I blame them. The end is concerning.

Detective Murphy: Did you hurt your family, Mr. Browne?

Jonathan Browne: No. I've saved them, Detective Murphy.

Detective Murphy: Let me try to make sure I understand everything you've told me. You've been having dreams for a week, right? Weird dreams about a fire coming and part of the human population transforming into moths so they can naturally float on up to the moon and escape humanity's flaming disintegration?

Jonathan Browne: Well, yes, but that's what I'm trying to tell people about. Overnight—tonight—the rest of the transformations will occur worldwide. Those of us left behind will have to protect our loved ones until the moon glows tomorrow night. If we just let them go now, there are too many clouds. They'll wind up zapped in bug fryers—

Detective Murphy: (*LAUGHING*) In bug fryers—

Jonathan Browne: Lost, and everything else. It's tomorrow night when we'll release them, and they'll go. It'll be beautiful. I'm telling you. It is in my dream. It is. The whole thing.

Detective Murphy: The next morning fire will destroy the remaining population?

Jonathan Browne: Yes. On the morning of the 20th.

Detective Murphy: You'll be destroyed?

Jonathan Browne: Yes.

Detective Murphy: Why you, Mr. Browne? Of all the humans in the entirety of this world, why would someone like you be chosen to deliver this message? A man who—

Jonathan Browne: Because why would anybody listen to a man like me?

Detective Murphy: Exactly. That's my question?

Jonathan Browne: Are you a man of faith, Detective Murphy?

Detective Murphy: Stop asking me that! Stop it! (*HAND SLAPS TABLE*)

(*KNOCK*)

Detective Mullins: Tom?

Detective Murphy: (*HEAVY BREATHING*) Yeah.

Detective Mullins: You might want to hurry it along.

Detective Murphy: I'm busy, Debbie.

Detective Mullins: Now, Tom.

Detective Murphy: Why?

Jonathan Browne: You shall take them and shall protect them until it is time for them to go safely on home. You shall take them and shall protect them—

Detective Murphy: Will you shut up, man? Please! (*HAND SLAPS TABLE*)

Detective Mullins: We are getting calls, Tom.

Detective Murphy: Calls?

Detective Mullins: I think you'll want to check them out.

Jonathan Browne: Are you a faithful man, Detective Murphy? A believer?

Detective Murphy: Shut up! Shut up!

(CHAIR SCRAPES AGAINST FLOOR)

Detective Mullins: Go home, Mr. Browne. We'll have to continue our questioning later.

Jonathan Browne: You shall take them and shall protect them—

Detective Murphy: I'll find out what you did with them! If it's the last thing I do, I will! *(UNINTELLIGIBLE)*

Jonathan Browne: You shall take them and shall protect them until it is time for them to go safely on home. You shall take them and shall protect them until it is time for them to go safely on home. You shall take them and shall protect them until it is time for them to go safely on home. You shall take them and shall protect them—

(DOOR SLAMS AGAINST FRAME)

2 TRUTHS & A LIE ABOUT THE MONSTERS ATOP OUR HILL

1.

There were monsters at the cave atop our hill. If not for the dragons' heavy shadows that blocked the sun, we might not have even
noticed them circling our cave, perhaps thinking their floating
smoky breaths were nothing more than astray cumulus clouds.

While we pointed from our lowly valley with a brand of
child-like wonder at the emerald-scaled pair overhead, Bob
Shaney shouted for us to stop.

To go inside.

Ready our bows.

Sharpen our swords.

He, sweating and swearing, insisted the newly-arrived dragons would kill us for no reason other than the simple fact that
they were, indeed, dragons. Monsters at heart.

We chuckled, softly, but he kept on with such a determined rage that our laughter wasted away into a brand of quiet doubt. Not in Bob, but in ourselves. In our fledgling belief that the dragons might have been good neighbors–perhaps even marvelous ones. That we might've ridden on their backs, gripping their blunted scales, to worlds we'd dreamed of. That they might've used their fire to help us clear brush for bountiful fields. That we might've made them pies from sweet berries they brought back to us from far-away journeys. But these were ridiculous whims.

Slowly, we turned away, heads down and silent, back to the shelter of our thatch-covered roofs.

Bob called out to a select few. The bravest pleaded to go with him at dusk, weapon clad, to the cave at the top of our hill.

"It's the only way," he insisted. "The only way."

We watched out our windows that very night as they went. Their blurry faces near memories already, we believed, with their glinting metal weapons and torches of flame mere faint embers in the distance.

2.

There were monsters at the cave atop our hill. We no longer doubted it. Not after Bob and our others returned, miraculously unharmed, the next morning with their job unfinished—and stories of what they'd witnessed.

"Too colossal," he said. "Nearly immortal."

"Enormous manifestations of pure evil," another added.

"Pointed tails and teeth sharper and harder than the lot of swords we carried."

We felt like fools for what we'd originally believed about the dragons—the monsters.

We vowed to help. To join together, as one, to complete the daunting task.

We spent the day preparing for revenge, only slowing for quick bites of food, not even taking the time to sit down with our neighbors and families. Our bellies were full of something else entirely.

We broke into groups. Some found stones. Others did the sharpening. A few packed sheaves.

As dusk approached, we gathered together. All of us. Men and women and children. And we marched, just like our own had the night before, with our weapons and fire to the top of our hill.

When we arrived at the cave–*our* cave–Bob yelled and screamed, and we did the same. Told the pair to come at us. To try again what they had the night before.

There was no wasted time. The dragons came, stepping slowly into the light of our flame. Immediately, we saw proof of the good fight our bravest had given.

Beautiful no more, the dragons' scales were cracked and bruised.

Blood oozed from holes against their ribs so much so that their skin didn't look green at all. But, instead, a dull gray.

Their wings, flat against their bodies, ripped and burnt.

Their talons were torn and loose from their claws.

The dragons didn't charge. They waited, silently asking us what we might do.

We ran to them, trying to finish the job from the night before.

We poked. Jabbed. Plunged.

The dragons cried out, but they didn't swat at us. Instead, for a time, they lazily pushed us aside. Seeming to beg us—plead for us—to stop. But we fought on.

Flaying them.

We drew them out into the open night, away from any protection our cave might've granted.

All that night, never once did the dragons use their fire, but they did try to gain flight. Several times they tried. Kicking against pebbles. Wings fluttering but failing.

But there was no escaping us.

3.

We are now a land free of monsters.

CLAIRE & HANK

I. Before.

I can remember when I was a little kid, maybe six or seven, how all of Dad's buddies used to make a fuss over Claire.

"Incredible."

"Astonishing."

"Absolutely miraculous."

Their words.

I constantly reminded them that a Pteranodon wasn't technically even a dinosaur, but they didn't care. She was a giant prehistoric bird with a wingspan greater than any four of them put together. And she could fly.

It's not like they ignored me during their visits. In fact, without fail, they'd summon me to their sides. "Hank," they said, and they waved me over. Each time, I'd feel the smallest flutter in the pit of my stomach, thinking it was finally going to be my moment, that they were going to ask me something about the world—about myself. But when I went to them, *always*, they patted my head and asked if I might fetch them another ice cream sandwich or a cold glass of Kool-Aid.

All afternoon and evening, Dad and his friends took turns holding Claire's leash, gazing at her, as she scooped down, harness-clad and all, into our pond to catch her own catfish dinner.

They had the best time watching her, too. Grown people squealing, laughing, and clapping because an ancient, human-sized bird with a toothless beak could fly and catch a few fish.

After I picked up all their sticky wrappers and crinkled cups, I sat on the bank and drew in the dirt or flicked pebbles at crickets. Anything to keep from looking up at her.

Dad was a paleontologist whose wife—my mother—had died during his only son's birth. Searching for reason, for evidence, for distraction was part of him. It wasn't so much in his blood; it was his blood.

On Christmas morning of 1981, instead of drinking hot chocolate or ripping the bow off my first bicycle, he dragged me out to excavate the far western corner of our backyard for fossils.

We were on our knees, tucked into one another to keep the cold wind from burning our faces. I held the flashlight, and Dad, with his hand shovel, dug as far into the cracked dirt as it would go, which was surprisingly far considering how it had been below freezing since the week after Thanksgiving.

Us prodding around in the dirt wasn't a special activity. We did it just about every day. Still, Dad got excited, and he grew especially excited anytime we actually found something. He'd start screaming at the discovery of an arrowhead, the skeleton of a field mouse, or a calcified dog turd.

When he started up howling on Christmas morning, I thought Spike, the Dalmatian from next door, had probably visited earlier in the week and left us a couple of treasures.

Unlike usual, though, Dad wouldn't stop shouting.

I was right beside him, but he hollered at me to bring the flashlight closer, and being the good son I was, I did what my father asked.

That was when I saw her, trapped in an enormous underground cave in our very own yard.

Dad wasn't alone in his yelling then. I shook so hard I smacked the flashlight against the dirt and caused the lens to shatter.

Dad didn't care. Truthfully, I don't think he noticed.

In a soft voice I didn't recognize as his, he started coaxing her out of her hole. "Come here, baby. Come on. I'll take good care of you," he whispered.

Claire didn't seem scared at all as Dad reached for her. She held up her almond-colored wings, and with a couple twists and one long tug, she was back above the soil.

I almost started yelling again, but when she was eye-level with me, I was too scared to make any sounds. Just hard nose breaths I couldn't help.

She squawked and strutted around for a bit, flapping clouds of dust and mites in my face.

I hoped Dad would cover me with his coat, but he didn't. Instead, he held out his hand for her to smell.

She went on up to him and rubbed her head against his calloused fingers.

That small sign of love—or maybe it was simple gratitude—was enough. He pushed me out of the way and led her inside our house like she was a newly-adopted golden retriever.

"How is she even alive?" I called breathlessly to him as he was opening the door.

"Miracle, son," he shouted, not even looking at me. "Maybe one of those oxygen bubbles. Don't matter how."

Then, he slammed the door.

∽♨⌇∾

Once I was finally able to breathe normally again, I went inside. He didn't give me any time to adjust. He told me I needed to give up my bedroom for a few nights—so Claire could have her own space to heal. A place she could make a nest and get comfortable.

Dad made me move out my few toys and clothes. I grabbed my pjs and sat on the worn plaid couch in the living room.

A terrible crash came from my bedroom. When I ran in to look, I saw Dad with a hammer and an ax, destroying my bed and dresser.

"Your sister might be able to use the wood somehow," he said.

"My sister?"

"Yes. Claire."

"Claire?"

"The Pteranodon."

"The Pteranodon?"

He didn't respond, so I walked back to the couch and sat down again, looking out at the snow beginning to fall.

He came to me a few minutes later and sat on the cushion beside me. "Be happy, Hankie. It's Christmas morning, and you've got yourself a new sister."

I rolled my shoulders.

"You should have some fun," he said, reaching into his back pocket and retrieving a pair of scissors. "Go cut up your mattress. She'll love nesting in those feathers."

I took his offering. I should have stabbed her and just dealt with the consequences from Dad right then, but I didn't. I did what he told me to do, trying the whole time to keep my tears to myself.

When January rolled around, Dad signed me out of school. He explained I needed to help care for Claire while he excavated the rest of the yard, looking for more Pteranodons. "Maybe we can have that big family I always dreamed of after all, Hankie," he said.

Instead of buying me textbooks—or even boring little kid books about sharing and friendship, he said I'd be learning "life skills." But there was a problem. The skills weren't so much for my own life. They were all about Claire's.

He showed me, for example, how to put on Claire's harness so she wouldn't fly away, which she had already tried to do at least a dozen times, and how much resistance to give her when she took flight.

After I mastered those two things, he taught me how to change her nest with newspapers each morning so she wouldn't have to sit on her own filth, how to walk her in the yard, and how to muzzle her when she got too loud.

All of this I learned before I could tie my own shoes or make a proper peanut butter and jelly sandwich.

School wasn't the only thing I had to give up because of her. My birthday presents soon went out the window. When August 17th rolled around each year, we took trips to a local park so Claire could get outside and fly around in big, open spaces on her Dad-made, duct tape and leather leash.

Dad finally got me some books to read for school after I was a couple of semesters behind, but they were all about birds, care-taking, and the prehistoric period. To make things even worse, they weren't kid-friendly versions either. I could only figure out (maybe) ten words on each page. "A." "The." "Bird." That was where I was.

I couldn't join the soccer team or play baseball because Dad said I had to make sure Claire was taken care of.

Even my television habits had to change because the bright animation I preferred made Claire screech and shred the carpet.

I began to dream about the day I'd turn eighteen. It was going to be when I could—would—finally escape Dad and Claire.

On the morning of my big day, I didn't even bother brushing my teeth. Or going to pee. Or brushing my hair. Or rubbing the sleep from my eyes.

I tore my blanket off, hopped up, slid on my shoes, and grabbed my plastic bags of clothes beside the couch—my couch—and I headed out the door.

The sun wasn't all the way up, but I could still see Dad.

He was hunched over dead in one of his holes in the front yard. Already a mix of gray and light blue. He was forty-nine.

II. After.

Before I called the funeral home, I went to my old bedroom, which I'll admit looked pretty cool with the mini-tree-house-looking space Dad had designed and painted, and I woke up Claire.

When I say I woke her up, what I mean is that I crept over to her nest and yanked one of her feathers real fast.

It's hard to say if she could understand English or not, so after I told her Dad was dead, I led her out there to sniff him. She started squawking and flapping her wings.

I took her back inside, where she flew to the couch and squatted, and I went to the kitchen and called the number in the phone book beside the Harris and Sons Mortuary Services listing.

Some old man answered on the first ring. I told him who I was and that Dad, Hank Sr., was dead in a hole of his own making in the yard.

He said he was sorry for my loss—of course—and he'd be out soon enough, but he made me promise "the Triceratops" would be locked up.

"She will be," I said, and I hung up the receiver.

Claire was glaring at me when I came back to the couch. Again, I'm not sure if she knew English, so I was a little scared by her look.

"Come on," I said, grabbing her harness. "Let's go for a walk in the yard."

Her expression softened as I fitted it on her and we went out the door.

We walked beside the fence in silence for a couple of minutes, but that quietness was just fueling my rage. I lost it on her. Like totally lost it. I started yelling how she'd taken my dad away. How she'd taken my room away. How she'd taken my whole childhood away. I was carrying on so hard I was kind of spitting on her as I was looking down at her.

I bent down and, with my shaking, fumbling hands, undid her harness. "Go on! Leave!"

She gave me that same look she'd given me on the couch, and she started raising her wings.

With a few good pushes, she was up in the air.

"Gone on!" I yelled. "I hate you!"

She didn't look back.

Claire didn't come back for the funeral, but everybody asked about her. Dad's buddies wanted to see her again. A couple of them had even brought her some catfish fillets wrapped in newspaper.

I told them she'd broken her harness because she was so sad about Dad and she'd left me just like he had. That hit them in the gut real good, I could tell.

They shoved the fish in my arms and said, before going to their cars, "In case she comes back."

For a couple of nights, I thought about eating her fish, but each time I went to the refrigerator and unwrapped it on the counter, I covered it up again and shoved it back on the shelf. I was that way about pretty much everything. When I went in my old room, ready to take it back, I shut the door. When I grabbed a pair of scissors, with the determination of tearing a certain harness into a million pieces, I placed them back in the drawer.

I couldn't sleep either. I laid awake, staring up at the ceiling and thinking about what I'd done to Claire. I started comparing how what I'd done to her was basically the same thing Dad had done to me.

I'd let her go.

I'd let her go, and I was all she had. All she knew. And she was helpless in the world.

I began having this recurring dream where I was walking out in the backyard at sunset, and when I looked up, there she was, flying back home. She landed right in front of me and dropped this ugly, fossilized, broken egg shell thing at my feet. I picked it up and inspected it. I can't exactly explain why, but in my dream, I imagined it was one of her eggs from millions of

years ago and she was telling me how badly she needed someone because, for her, there was no one else but me. Then, I
hugged my sister, and when I wrapped my arms around her
neck, it wasn't with the thought of breaking it in half. It was to
let her know I was sorry and could see we were both hurt. And
together, maybe, somehow, we would be okay.

But, yeah, that was only a dream.

After I got all of Dad's affairs settled, I thought about leaving
like I'd originally planned, but I didn't. Instead, I picked up his
shovel and took to the rest of the unexplored yard, searching for
something I'd never find.

DO YOU REMEMBER?

Mom, do you remember the photo from our only family trip to the beach? The one Dad took of you? The one where you look untamed? Maybe even free? Whole?

Do you remember the day the photo was taken? The wind tickling our skin? The birds singing overhead? The soft rain washing all of our pain away? Us laughing at the feeling of the squishy sand between our toes?

Do you remember the beachgoers screaming and running when they saw me? How we tried not to notice? How you begged me to try my best not to? How, only a few minutes after our arrival, all of the sand and water we could see was ours?

Do you remember how, then, we stood at the edge of the water and allowed the waves to roll into our ankles? How we stood surrounded by milky jellyfish corpses and broken shells and watched for fins? Ones like mine? And how I spotted one? Then a dozen? How I couldn't stop crying? And how you hugged me? And you refused to let go? Do you? Do you, Mom?

Do you remember how hard you worked so we could be there? How you saved all of your tips from your shifts at the diner so I could, for once, see others who looked (*almost*) like me? How you saved and saved so I could have that experience of not being alone in the world, even if that company could only last for three days and two nights? Even if we had to sleep in that one bed? Even if there were holes in the wall? Even if the sink didn't drain? And the bathtub didn't fill?

Do you remember when Dad finally came out of the hotel room to join us? How we couldn't believe it? How we ran to him? And how he backed away, but we pretended not to notice? How you asked him to take the photo? Your photo on the beach? On our beach? How, almost as soon as the flash went off, and we had the memory for forever, the rain came harder? How the wind let loose? How the waves knocked you over and you hurt your knees? How you couldn't get up and the water lapped over you? How you started coughing? Choking?

Do you remember how I tried to help? Me running to you on my thin, seven-year-old human legs? Nudging you with my tiny fins? With the rubbery tip of my nose? Me opening wide so you could grab onto one of my teeth? How helping you actually made it worse? How I cut you? How I made you bleed?

Do you remember how scared you were of me? How it was you crying? And not me? How you were pleading? Begging? Because my nose was twitching? My pupils were dilating?

Do you remember how you squeezed your cut hand into your other one? Your clean one? Your perfect one? The one you had just tucked into mine a few minutes earlier when we'd walked along the shoreline? How you, seeing that hand could not help, dunked your bleeding one into the water? Shielded it with the rest of your body? Protected it with everything you had?

Do you remember how the sharks came to you? The entire shiver of sharks we'd spotted earlier on the horizon? Do you remember how they nipped at you? How they snapped at your body? How they tried to drag you away?

Do you remember how they looked at me when I got between them and you? What they did when they really saw me? All of me? How they ducked their heads back into the water? Their bodies straightened? Their fins went away? How fast they vanished?

Do you remember how Dad yelled at you to get up? At you to see what sharks were really like? What I would become? What I already was?

Do you remember how he stood so far away? And how he told us he couldn't do it anymore? That he was done? That he left us alone, out in the bloody water, to drown?

Do you remember, Mom, how I finally got you up? How I saved you? How I wedged your legs into my mouth and spat you on the sand? How I only gave you a few new cuts? How you cried and cried all night on the far side of our bed? How I told you, over and over and over again, we would both be okay?

DYING AT ALLIUM FARM

I'm dangling a rabbit above my mouth when my mother shines her spotlight-shaming flashlight in my face. "You don't have to be so obvious about it, Anna," she says, snatching my snack and tossing it across the lantern-lit field.

"Who cares?" I say. "I'm leaving anyway."

"You aren't going anywhere. Our family has run this farm for over two centuries, and you're one of us whether you want to be or not. Now get up, and start picking the bags of garlic scapes like I asked."

"Whatever. I hate this stupid place."

Mom doesn't reply. Instead, she huffs and leaves, kicking rocks down the farm's perfectly symmetrical rows until she's lost among the night's shadows.

Other than draining various small animals, there isn't a lot to do for fun in our little Tennessee hellhole, a town that hosts such regular activities as demolition derbies, cow-tipping gatherings, and cookie-decorating competitions.

It's especially awful for someone like me, who is an aspiring intellectual. And a vampire.

The townsfolk here, unsurprisingly, don't know the vampire part. My grandma, June, who I so *lovingly* call "Junie June," has been running Allium Farm since she and Mom came over from Romania, which was probably before the wheel was invented, but nothing gives her—or us—away. Not her age. Not the farm's "convenient" hours of 5 PM until 6 AM. Not the fact that we wear gloves every single time we handle our "prized" garlic. Not the fact that when Junie June smiles, her two comically-long fangs catch at her old, saggy, reversed-chestnut-looking lips and just hang there all guiltily. Never mind that there is almost always a crimson stain from some kind of unlucky animal just begging for attention.

I'm serious, too, about how stupid the people are here. A few months back, I set my profile picture on all of my social media accounts to be the one of me sucking the blood from the biggest rabbit I've ever seen. In the photo, you can see literal blood dripping onto my lips. And you know what? One of our longest customers, Irma Applegate, who I swear looks as old as Junie June, said, at the end of one of my shifts last week, "Oh, Anna. Your picture on the computer is so cute. You kids really enjoy your Halloween." I smiled the biggest fake smile I could muster, showing her every bit of my fangs. I know they were glinting in the first blinding slivers of the sunrise, but she—she just laughed.

I swear, if rabbits weren't such breeding machines, Irma Applegate would already be dead. That repulsive, moronic woman asks me at least twice a week where the "freshest, coldest, most delicious garlic" is. We have never remodeled any-thing. Honestly, nothing has changed or moved or been altered in any kind of way. The two-door display refrigerator is probably a part of the concrete slab it sits on by now.

Mom and Junie June would stake me if they knew this, but I keep my first edition of *Dracula* in my back pocket dur-ing my shifts. When I see customers approach, I pull it out and start reading—just to see if any switch goes off in these idiots' pea-brains, but nothing comes of it except for weird comments. "I wish I had time to read." "Never heard of that one, but the cover is cute."

When I get back from the field, I put the bags of garlic scapes under the counter and wink at Mom, who is helping the last few customers of the morning at the register.

There are three dead rabbits under the counter already. I guess I should be happy she didn't kill me, but I'm not.

I take that back. I look forward to leaving here. I have to be alive for that to happen.

I crave the coming days of *real* schooling. Not the kind I'm used to, which is full of *alleged* teachers—coaches—rambling on about conspiracy theories they believe are facts and peers—a word I'm using very loosely—who can't tell the difference between a subject and a verb and who go on and on about my "stinking" lunch and my "gothic" sunglasses and long-sleeve shirts.

I dream about my upcoming days full of peer-reviewed essays. Allegorical novels. Morality plays. Works of translation. Intellectual discussions. Actual respect.

I can almost feel a smile forming on my face, but I catch myself before I do anything that stupid. I do the smart thing instead. I sit there in my blood-soaked shirt and greet all of our fine customers.

Mom snarls at me when the man at the register looks down to unlatch his camouflage wallet. She is good with the customers. Smiling. Laughing. Giving them their change. Pretending she doesn't dream about bathing in the filling from their veins.

"Y'all have a good one," I say as I head into our house, which conveniently functions as the farm's storage area.

Inside, Junie June is in my half-closed coffin with her teeth plunged into a deer leg. She's sucking so hard that her cheeks look like deflated balloons. She glances over at me from behind the oaken lid and says, "I'm dying, Anna."

As if to prove her honesty, she drops the leg and lifts up her shirt to show me the blisters all over her nearly-translucent body.

I choke from repugnance.

"You can't just show me all that, Junie June," I say between spurts of air.

"The sun has taken its toll," she says, tossing the coffin lid to the ground and pushing past me on her way to the refrigerator to get a glass of her bedtime nectar, which, disgustingly, isn't blood, but buttermilk.

I watch her for a few minutes as she pours herself a giant glass. She doesn't look back at me. She just utters the most horrible six-word phrase I've ever heard: "I am leaving you the farm."

I scream.

Junie June's glass explodes.

I keep screaming.

She doesn't flinch. Instead, she goes over to the tiny cabinet that's off one of its hinges, and she gets down the peanut butter. Junie June plunges her fingers inside, scoops up a handful, and flings it into her mouth. She chews it and doesn't even try to close her mouth.

Last week, Mom said to me, "Anna, Mrs. Applegate is one of our best customers. She said you told her to—umm—'F' off when she asked if you could help her find an item. You didn't really tell that old woman that, did you?" I gave her the same response, just so she'd know the truth.

Clearly, I'm not the kind of person who has an interest in owning a small business. Especially in such a *small* place.

"I. Don't. Want. The. Farm," I insist. "Leave it to Mom."

Junie June walks, brushing against me, over to her coffin, still not looking at me. "Your mother is dying too," she says, slobbering brown, crunchy goop.

It surprises me that I don't feel anything when she delivers the news.

"You don't mean dying as in dead?" I say. "You mean dying as in hiberhealing?"

Junie June swallows her horrible snack and finally makes eye contact. When she does, she laughs at me. "Yes, you foolish girl. Hiberhealing for ten years or so to let these nasty spots go away so I—we—don't explode and die as in dead. Our customers do love us, but they can't wait on us for over a decade to get their organic garlic."

"Well, I'm not doing it. I told you that I'm getting out of here as soon as I graduate from high school next year. I'm going to college—Wesleyan, preferably—to do something with my life."

"You shouldn't try to outgrow your raising. Besides, the university in the county over is the best in the state. I'm sure you can get a full scholarship. School AND work together, my naïve granddaughter. You don't want that student debt. I listen to the news."

"I am not going to any university within a thousand miles of this small-minded place."

She laughs obnoxiously, and she keeps laughing as she gets another glass of buttermilk ready. She doesn't go silent until she chugs her drink.

Once the buttermilk's coated her throat in the sour film she craves, she turns her back to me and starts hysterically laughing again—like she never stopped—and goes back to her coffin and steps inside.

Just when she's about to fasten herself in for what seems like a long, loooooong sleep, she steps back out and marches over to me. Her tiny, wobbly head barely reaches the height of my navel, and I can feel her breath puffing through the cotton fabric that covers my stomach. She takes her left index finger and starts jabbing me. All over. As hard as she can. Over and over again.

I step back, and when I'm cornered into the wall, I leap away from her and run to the other side of the room. She chases me. Junie June, who can barely manage to scuttle most days, *flies* after me, plunging her old, bony, blistery fingers into every part of me that she can reach. "I said I'm leaving you the farm, and I don't care what you want to do or don't want to do."

Mom swings the door back and lunges between us, shielding me the best she can. Honestly, she's too thin to block much, but it's the thought that counts. "Stop! Stop!" she yells.

Junie June jabs her just as hard as she does me. Her fingers like knives. Or more like old, chipped spoons in her case, the way she bites her nails.

I start back. "I don't want the farm! I don't want the farm! I don't want the farm! I HATE THIS PLACE!"

We don't stop until Irma Applegate walks in. "Excuse me," she says all polite-like, but no one is into that. Not after we close for the morning. She can obviously tell, so she joins our raging ensemble.

"June!" she shouts. "Jesus have mercy! Stop this nonsense at once!"

When we don't stop, she yanks her purse off her shoulder and starts whaling us. She aims for Junie June, but she's not much of a shot. The cabinets take most of the licks. The purse isn't zipped, so lipsticks, used tissues, and peppermints go flying. One of the mints ricochets off my tooth and breaks in two. The smaller chunk lands in Mom's mouth and lodges in the pipe it shouldn't, choking her.

Although the purse is empty, Irma takes it and starts spanking Junie June. She even lands a few swings. One grandma whooping another with a useless purse.

I'm low-key mad at Mom for trying to catch her breath. The way she jerks about interrupts my line of sight.

Finally, Junie June abates. "What is it, Irma? You nosy coot! This is family business. Can't you see that we've closed?"

"I'm sorry, June!" Irma says. "You'll have to forgive me. I got carried away with the time. I know it's past close. But I need some of the freshest, coldest, most delicious garlic you have to finish off Howard's morning oatmeal, honey, and cinnamon concoction that he likes so much, and I couldn't quite remember where it is. I was hoping someone could point me in the right direction. So—I—well, I thought I'd come in here and see if I could get some assistance."

I can't handle it. I just can't. I fly into her and rip her neck open, sucking every ounce of my favorite sweet crimson juice I can get.

I'm just kidding. I actually yell, "I'm not taking the farm!" "I'm not taking the farm!" "I'm not taking the farm!"

Mom gulps and finally swallows Irma's mint.

Irma stares at me, and her cheeks go red. I can't tell if she's embarrassed or angry or just hot from the quarrel. "What do you mean you aren't taking the farm? What's happening to it?"

"I'm dying," Junie June says, lifting her shirt to show off her blistered body. Again.

"And I'm not far behind," Mom adds. She starts to lift her shirt, but I grab her hand and put it back at her side.

"We believe you," I say. "BOTH of you."

Irma starts crying. "Sweet heavens. My precious June and Helen! Cancer! You both have cancer!"

I feel sort of guilty that no one corrects her, but explaining hiberhealing wouldn't really be an option.

"Howw. Cannn. Youuuu. Nottttt. Wantttttt. Alliummm-mmmmm. Farmmmmmmmmmm?" Irma asks, sobbing in a dramatic crescendo. She composes herself well enough to zip out one quick sentence that sounds more like a word. "ThisplaceismyfavoritebusinessinallofTennessee!"

"I don't want Allium Farm!" I shout at Irma. "I hate everything about it and every person who lives in this awful town."

"But why don't you want it?" Irma asks, apparently (and unsurprisingly) unable to use context clues.

I compose myself and repeat my plain reasoning as calmly as I can, "I hate everything about it and every person who lives in this awful town."

"How can you hate your home?"

Mom and Junie June don't bother to jump in. It's as if they have suddenly transformed into two human bobble-heads, the way they bounce their necks along with the conversation. One corner to the next. And back again.

"Well, let me see," I say, peering at Mom and Junie June before I look back at awful Irma. "There is no culture here. Like at all. Do you even know what the Neoclassical literary period is? Or, here's an easy one for you, the Renaissance? When I mention the Romantics, does that mean anything to you? Of course not—not to anyone in this shoebox of a town. AND I'm tired of the comments about my books. I'm tired of no one else *reading* books. I'm tired of the nasty words about my lunch and my clothing. I'm tired of all of it! You people—you—you don't even know we are—"

"Vampires," Irma interjects.

Although all three of us are about as pale as it gets already, we go full on transparent when she says it.

Irma smirks as she goes to the counter and hops up on it. When she lands, she lets out an enormous fart that rattles the walls and makes me nearly lose my balance. It doesn't phase her. She doesn't twist her face or scrunch her nose or anything. That's how in control she is.

Junie June taps Mom's shoulder and points at the window. Mom runs to open it and, quicker, darts back to her place to watch the impending showdown.

"Of course I know what you all are, girlie," Irma says.

"Every person around knows it. A garlic farm? *Really*? And guess what? Nobody cares. People around here don't even own stakes—not anymore. And no, we might not read big, fancy books, but not all people have the same interests. I, for instance, like my nice, little Christmas movies that come on all year on my favorite cable channel—I can't think of what it's called, but I bet you if I called my Howie, he could tell you. He hands me the remote every night and tells me to enjoy my picture. And I do, Anna. I enjoy it always. You might not realize this about yourself, but you aren't the easiest person to talk to. And your family—your precious family has always been good to us. To the whole community. June and Helen support the elementary school. They've probably donated a thousand pounds of garlic for our 'Back to School Spaghetti Supper' fundraisers over the years. So, we support them—and you—in return," she says.

She waits a few seconds to allow her words to settle. Then, she hops down.

Junie June and Mom turn into each other and give each other a timid high-five. I scowl at them, but they turn their attention to Irma, who has her sight set on me.

She pulls a wet ten-dollar bill out of her bra and tosses it over her shoulder. It drops, like it weighs as much as a bowling ball, and smacks the floor. "For the garlic," she says.

Finally deciding it's time to acknowledge stray sounds, she lets out an "oops" as she crunches one of the peppermints that litters the floor.

She walks over to Mom and Junie June and almost hugs them, but she steps back, just as she's about to go forward, and takes hold of their hands instead. "I will miss both of you dearly," she says.

"And we you, Mrs. Applegate. You have always been one of our favorite customers," Mom says, lying.

"Will you watch our girl?" Junie June asks. "Make sure she's okay?"

"I promise," Irma says as she turns and smiles at me.

"I haven't said I'm taking the farm," I say. "I have my own plans. Leaving. Getting out of here."

All three of them start to laugh so loudly that they can hardly breathe. Irma, of course, is howling, her back arching and her arms swinging. It's like she's doing an impromptu performance that is a full-on embracement of the embarrassment that is postmodern dance. "She sure is something. These kids these days and their big dreams," she says.

Irma finally heads out the door, but almost as soon as she does, she's back inside, peeking her head inside the open window. "Oh, Anna. I'll pick up the garlic that I just paid for when I come back this evening."

I flip her off, but it's too late. She's already rounded the window frame.

As the sun starts to rise, shining through the window, I tell Mom and Junie June what they want to hear. "Fine," I say. Once the word leaves my lips, I go in my coffin and begin to shut the door, but I jut my head out for one last thing. "I want you both to know that I'm going to a private university as far away from here as I can find, as soon as one of you is better. I mean it, too. I have to get away, if it's the last thing I do."

Neither Mom nor Junie June offers support as I close my coffin. After a little sleep, I'll go to school and dream about my future. Come evening, I'll go out in the field and start my shift.

REMEMBRANCE DAY

I'm first in line for Remembrance Day. I've been here since midnight. The announcement never said what time the gates would open—just that it would be early. Although the clouds are heavy, it's nearly sunrise. The entrance's wooden gate isn't as solid as it used to be, so I peek inside. There are dozens of workers. Each one carefully walks the grounds and finds a home behind a projector. These men work meticulously, connecting cords and flipping switches. With each flip, a lively holograph appears. Most of the hazy forms are recalled bodies of the old. Gray hair. Sunken faces. But there are a few kids. Small and lost in innocence.

I turn where I know Caleb should be, and I see him. My Caleb. My beloved son. I hold up my hand to wave, but I catch myself and stop.

Still, I watch him. He vanishes, but he appears again. The process repeats. It's supposed to be this way at first.

"Welcome to Remembrance Day," a man says as he unlatches the lock. He stands at the entrance and pauses, taking time to clear his throat. "Folks, what you are about to witness has taken me over fifty years to develop. Death isn't what it used to be. And you'll see that now," he says. His voice is jovial and proud. He scoots to the side, clearing the path. All of the families behind me clap and howl as they enter the cemetery.

I don't. I run to my son.

I call out his name as I sprint toward him. He turns to me and darts in my direction. Even with the worker handling the projector, Caleb still cuts in and out.

When I get to him, I put my arms around his holograph and squeeze, but I only grasp air as my arms entangle themselves and collapse by my sides.

He looks up at me, and I stare back at him. His eyes. His face.

"I've missed you so much," I say.

He nods. Then, he pats his chest and points at me.

"They can't speak," the worker behind the projector says, smiling.

I shrug my shoulders.

"I love you, Caleb," I say. My boy smiles.

We go to his grave and sit down. I tell him about the past year. His baseball team. Roscoe, his Labrador. How I hung up all of his drawings. Even about how I sometimes play with his toys in his room. I ask if that's okay, and he nods.

We sit for a long time. All the families do.

The same worker who made the welcome speech taps my arm. He is different now. Sterner. Colder. "It's time to leave, sir,"

he says, not looking at me. "Technology won't hold up much longer. Might be too much for you."

I thank him and stand up.

Caleb gets up as I do, and he tries to hug me. His arms float around my body and collapse into broken pixels. He shakes his head.

"It's okay, buddy," I tell him. This time, I press my hand to my chest and, then, point at him.

His mouth moves. I don't have to hear the words to know what he's saying.

"I'll see you again," I say.

I walk away and turn back to look at Caleb, but he's already gone. They all are—the living and the dead.

Remembrance Day is over.

PEACHES' MENAGERIE

Peaches sat alone on her front porch. Although the rain splattered against her face and onto her thick, gray-rimmed glasses, she didn't go inside. She insisted on greeting the child. There had been no phone calls or letters announcing the arrival. Still, she knew, so she waited.

Her oak rocker moved with the storm's wind.

Soon, the rain fell harder. The thunder wasn't far behind.

Peaches rose. Her strong bare feet dug into the planks as she sauntered to the steps. Her hands gripped the slippery railing as she moved toward the grass.

She walked until she stood under the lone light in her yard. The wind whipped the loose bulb against the beaten pole. Her skin, soaked with rain, glittered in the darkened yard. She folded her arms across her waist and waited, peering through the thicket for the first sign of outside life.

An owl hooted above Peaches, and she looked up into the storm.

"Come, Zora" she said. And Zora did. Her wings extended as she glided onto the woman's shoulder. "So, you've come to see our new one, too?" she asked.

Zora blinked.

The nearby puddles enveloped Peaches' feet, but she remained firmly planted. Then, she saw something beyond the sheets of rain. "Look," she said to Zora.

The car slowly came to a stop. The temporary caretakers jumped out with the baby already in their arms. "Sahar," the woman called her.

"She was separated. Please take care of her—with the others," the man said softly. He stretched his arms away from his body as he held the baby out to Peaches.

Sahar's button nose wiggled, and her eyes closed as the rain blew into her face. Her appearance seemed peaceful. Then coughs, angry and determined, spouted from her small body. Her cheeks flushed.

Zora chirped, but the man paid the high-pitch sound no attention.

Peaches nodded and took the tiny child. She brushed Sahar's forehead and felt the heat. Her hands confirmed what she already knew.

Sahar immediately vomited onto Peaches' drenched body. The woman held the young girl and rubbed her back. "It's okay, my child. You are loved," she said softly.

The man ran back to his car and returned with a fuzzy brown bear. A button rested on the edge of its snout, and knotted, golden fabric served as eyes. He held it to Sahar's face and roared.

Sahar didn't face the man any longer; instead, her eyes were upon Peaches.

"Here," he said, tucking the creature into Peaches' cradled arm.

The caretakers ran back to their car, and they began to drive away, but at the edge of the driveway, their brake lights flashed. The redness glared so intensely that it lit up the front of the small house.

The menagerie was awake and on the move.

Zora flew from Peaches' shoulder and joined her friends.

Peaches rushed with Sahar to the door.

It was almost time.

Inside, Peaches removed Sahar's wet blanket. The baby cried as she rested naked on the soft cushions under the warm light.

Her quick breaths came as rattles, and spit ran down her pale chin.

Her fading eyes followed Peaches, who dampened a warm cloth under the nearby faucet.

Peaches, with a husky voice, began to sing to Sahar. She danced all the way to the dying baby, and when she reached Sahar, she held the child's small hand.

"You are loved," Peaches said in a singsong voice. "You are so, so loved, my beautiful, beautiful friend."

Sahar kicked her legs, and she smiled.

Peaches took the cloth and softly caressed Sahar's tiny body.

The end was coming. Sahar's breaths came quicker. Her body moved slower.

Peaches went to her dresser and removed a white blanket. She unfolded it and smoothed the wrinkles. She took the soft cotton and carefully dressed Sahar. When Sahar was secure, Peaches grabbed the plush bear and placed it beside the ailing baby. "Yours," she said, and she planted a kiss on Sahar's nose.

"Rest, my friend," Peaches whispered. "You will need your strength."

Peaches pulled up a chair to Sahar's side. She took the baby's hand into her own again and softly hummed.

Zora appeared at the window. "Already?" Peaches asked. The owl hooted softly in reply.

Soon, the other animals were watching. Their eyes glowing behind the glass, waiting on Sahar to join them. Eager. Ready.

"You are loved. You are so, so loved," Peaches repeated, while rubbing Sahar's fragile hands.

The words floated throughout the room, never landing. They swirled and swirled, wrapped in kindness and in love. Nothing was to settle. Not on this night. Instead, something was building. Something was growing.

When Peaches was seven, her sister, Zora, was born. Zora had a deformity. Her heart rested outside of her ribcage, and her veins pumped diseased blood.

"Your sister won't live past her first birthday," Peaches' mother said, shoving the baby into her small arms. "You take care of her. Your daddy needs my attention."

Peaches' father laughed and grabbed his wife's hand. He led her back to their bedroom and slammed the door.

Peaches held Zora and looked into her eyes—full and glowing. Baby Zora giggled and smiled, with her pink gums sparkling under the light. Peaches kissed her sister's soft forehead. "Don't you worry," she said. "You are my sister, and I'm going to love you for always."

Peaches grabbed the stuffed owl that the hospital's nurses had given her parents when Zora left their care, and she opened the door and left.

Her aunt and uncle lived down the road. They would assist her, she thought. They could help give Zora a good life.

When Peaches knocked on their door, her aunt quickly appeared. "Yes?" the woman asked. She wiped flour onto the towel that dangled from her waist. "Is that your mother's new child?"

"This is my sister, Zora," Peaches said, pulling the blanket from her head and showing the baby to her aunt.

But her aunt stepped back and moved her hand to cover her mouth. She turned and slammed the door. "She's not right!" she yelled. "Go on back home. A child doesn't have any business being out with a sick baby like that."

Peaches remained on the steps. She shouted through the wooden door, "Mama says she won't take care of her."

Peaches' aunt cracked the door and peeked her head out slightly. "Respect your mother."

Then, the door shut again, and Peaches listened as her aunt's heavy steps faded in the distance.

Peaches' grandmother was dead long before Peaches ever entered the world, but her house still stood. Peaches had been there once to get a few pots and pans with her mother.

"We're going to sleep in the field tonight, Zora," she said to her sister, caressing her few strands of curly hair. "Then, we're going up that hill tomorrow," she said, pointing off in the distance. "We're going to our own home."

Peaches took Zora, and, under the bright moonlight, they rested in the open field.

She held Zora closely by her side and drifted into a dream.

It was her grandmother who came. Peaches knew without knowing, as she often did. Her grandmother's old hands, wrinkled and soft, reached down to her shoulders and then her back. She squeezed. A hug. Peaches hadn't been embraced in years, but it felt real in the dream. "Keep going, and keep loving," she said. Her grandmother's face came closer. "After you get there, it won't be long."

Peaches shook her head. Tears fell from her eyes. Her only sister would soon die. "But you take that owl you have, and you put it at Zora's feet when her time comes. You have a gift. You're leading a revolution, darling. You are the one to set this world right."

Peaches nodded, but she remained silent. Her grandmother's figure began to fade. Dust. Leaves. Clouds. She was all of those things now. Still her voice came. "Always keep your heart, and use my house to hold the menagerie until they are ready. They'll tell you. You just listen—you just love."

Peaches jumped awake. The tears were real. Her face was wet and her eyes swollen. The sun still hid under the horizon, but she grabbed Zora and charged toward the hill. Sweat ran down her face and every part of her body. She didn't stop until she was there.

When she stood in front of the house, her heart jumped. For the first time in her short life, Peaches felt like she was home.

The days and weeks passed quickly. Zora laughed and squirmed for more of the days than she didn't. It was only in her last week that she truly hurt.

The end came on a stormy night. The light flickered and the wind slammed against the loose windowpanes.

Peaches thought back to the dream in which her grandmother had visited her. She grabbed the owl and wedged it between Zora's tiny feet. She stood over her sister's body and kissed her soft cheek. Zora's head snuggled against her face, and she held her small hand. "You are so, so loved," Peaches said.

In the morning, the stuffed owl was gone. Zora's limp human body was where it had been—unmoved and undisturbed.

Peaches walked around her grandmother's house searching for the owl. She wondered what her grandmother had intended for her to do. She searched the floor, and she looked in all of the house's corners. Perhaps a stray burst of wind had knocked it to the ground.

She was on her knees, peering under a table, when the tap came at the window.

She looked up and began to cry.

"Zora," she said, and she ran to open the window.

Peaches grabbed the stuffed bear and moved it to Sahar's feet. She covered both child and bear with a blanket and went outside to tend to the menagerie behind her house. Her lingering love would do the work.

The animals allowed Sahar's caretakers' car to pass. Still, they had given the two humans quite the show.

They roared, and they charged.

They knocked over trees, and they kicked up grass.

They splattered mud in the sky, and they flashed their teeth when the lightning crackled.

When Peaches visited later, they were back in their shelter—calm, resting.

She brushed their thick hides with firm brushes, and she washed their backs and legs with warm water.

She brought treats for them. Peanuts for the elephant. Leaves for the giraffe. Exotic grass for the zebra. Meat for the tiger, lion, alligator, and hippo. Rodents for Zora.

Peaches sang to them—the same way she did when they were sick, when they were human.

She laughed, observing how the weakest children became the strongest animals.

Sahar's roar woke her. It woke all of the animals. They leapt from their beds and looked at the towering bear before them.

Sahar moved quickly along the fence, and she called out again.

She tore at the trees, with her claws ripping away the bark.

Peaches approached Sahar. "My child," she said softly.

Sahar's eyes looked down at Peaches.

"My child," Peaches continued. "Is it time?"

The other members of the menagerie stayed behind their mother—waiting, listening.

Peaches spoke again. Her voice loud and strong—roaring like the animals surrounding her.

"Is it time?" she shouted.

The animals, together now, answered in unison.

Their calls filled the morning dawn, and the ground trembled.

Sahar bent down, and Peaches crawled onto the giant bear's back.

"It is time!" Peaches called.

She held her arm toward the sky, and she roared.

They all did.

Peaches and her menagerie charged down the hill, ready to claim their world.

FROM 1973

1973.

"Okay, Henderson," the preacher said without looking up, squinting his eyes to focus on his handwritten notes that were nearly gone to shadows from standing under the old magnolia tree. "Repeat after me. I, Henderson Jackson, will love you, Cali Horton, in the good times and in the bad ones, and I will love you in times of sickness and in times of health, too—until death do us part."

Henderson opened his mouth to try to give it a fair attempt, but he didn't make it as far as reciting his name before his own laughter interrupted him. The thing with Henderson was that once he got going, he couldn't much stop. So, he laughed. Then, he laughed some more. And since, again, it was his very nature, he just kept going. He even swatted his knee and took his hat off and held it to his belly, his throat tilted up to the clouds.

The preacher blushed. "What's so funny?" he whispered to the man in front of him.

Henderson, still trying to catch his breath, coughed out, "Preacher, a little thing like death isn't going to make me stopping loving this here woman beside me. Ain't nothing doing us part. We already decided that one."

Cali tried to calm her own soft chuckle, which had begun at Henderson's mentioning of the word "death," that stirred from underneath her veil.

The preacher, a quiet, timid man, managed to muster a soft "I see." He didn't repeat himself with getting the vows right. Instead, he went ahead and declared the two in front of him man and wife, and then he took off to his Chevy, gone before the couple unclasped from their kiss.

Henderson and Cali danced all night under the glowing full moon. His family looked on. Hers there in spirit. Coyotes howled in the distance. Leaves floated around them. Fireflies twirled about. The two lovers didn't much notice any of it. They had each other now, and that wouldn't ever change.

2014.

Henderson and Cali sit high above the river, up next to the bridge, with their legs and feet dangling over it all—the ripples, the broken branches and towers of jagged rocks, the fish-starved birds.

She holds his free hand inside hers. Henderson's other one is busy clutching a stained handkerchief to his mouth. Although neither say anything about it, they both know it won't be long.

"I should've just stayed at home," he tells her.

He stops talking for a long while—long enough for him to catch his breath.

Cali hands him his jug of water, just like she's always done. Not always with water necessarily, but with water or pumpkin muffins or lost socks or love.

Cali hasn't aged like her husband. Her skin is still tight. Her breaths strong. Her hair as brown as the day they met.

"I'm not exactly who you think I am," she used to say to him, offering a clue as to why.

"I think you are my girl," is all he would ever say.

How could she argue with a man like that? A man who loved her more than anything else.

As a couple, it was him who experienced the signs of aging. In his forties, he lost his hair. In his fifties, he had a heart scare. In his sixties, it was cancer that struck him and never stopped striking.

"I'm just glad it's me." That was his response, and Cali would wrap her arms around him and squeeze.

After all of these years—forty-one married—she hasn't ever found the right moment to tell him.

At the water's edge, Cali asks Henderson if he is sure he loves her. If he knows for certain that he always will.

"You will always be my girl," he says, smiling at her.

She kisses his cheek, causing him to go into another coughing fit.

As he shakes and rattles, choking on his own mix of phlegm, blood, and who knows what else, Cali grabs Henderson, and she pushes him as hard as she can—so hard that he flies off the cliff.

His eyes meet hers on his way down, and it's in the exact moment before his head slaps against the rocks that he gets it.

⟡

In only a few seconds, Henderson joins his wife again, and, together, they watch the sun go down.

"I thought our forever should go ahead and get started. Was tired of watching you suffer."

"When did it happen to you?" he asks. "How did it happen? How did I not know?"

Cali gazes into his eyes and reaches for his hand. "Did you notice that you haven't coughed?"

Henderson nods, feeling like he did on the day he married Cali.

She reaches for his hand. "Come with me," she says.

They fly through all that is and was, seeing family members gone from long ago. Beloved pets they shared. Lost friends. Memories of two lives fully lived together.

They only stop when they are back under the familiar magnolia tree. He's wearing his hat and his best pair of cowboy boots, and she's in her flowing dress, the veil already gone. The wind is cool, and the grass whistles below them.

Unable to tell if he's remembering the past or if he's living the present, he asks Cali if she wants to dance.

She leans into him, and they hold one another tightly. Slowly, they sway.

He moves his mouth to her ear. "Nothing will do us part," he whispers.

"Nothing," she says.

NANCY R. MELSON'S STATE ELA EXAM, SECTION 1: THE DEAD-DEAD MONSTER

Directions: Read the informational essay about the Dead-Dead Monster and answer the following questions. Mark all of your answers in the testing booklet. Once finished, continue to the writing portion of the exam.

A Good Monster is NOT Hard to Find
by Liz Cornelius

1. The Dead-Dead Monster is one of the most popular cryptids of Alabama folklore. This creature, as documented by those who have allegedly encountered it, has an appearance comparable to that of a malnourished, **bipedal** wolf, with mange. In multiple interviews conducted by staff of the Clarisville Times, Alabama's oldest and most-circulated daily newspaper, supposed eyewitnesses further detail the

Dead-Dead Monster as measuring approximately seven feet tall, possessing an elongated snout, and accessorizing, most always, with a black top hat. Each of these very same interview subjects spoke of the Monster's **vile** stench and its hauntingly red, glowing eyes.

2. This cryptid certainly seems horrific, but in this case, looks might just be deceiving.

3. The first mention of the Dead-Dead Monster occurred in 1864, when a cholera outbreak ravaged Clarisville County. Thomas Williamson, who was twelve years old at the time, knew of the disease on a very personal level. Records indicate that, in Williamson's home county alone, 119 people died from cholera within a two-month span. Williamson's mother, father, and five siblings were among the unfortunate victims, but Williamson, who also contracted the intestinal infection, recovered. He owed his very survival to none other than the Dead-Dead Monster. In a recently discovered interview with Hiram Smith, a local journalist at the time, Williamson said, "I didn't want to die. I thought that was exactly what was happening when this huge, wolf-like creature that called itself the Dead-Dead Monster first came into our cabin and sat on the edge of my bed. But instead of leading me into the afterlife, it started singing to me. The lyrics were rather queer, but its voice was beautiful. Like some kind of low-pitched lullaby. The Dead-Dead Monster said if I really wanted to keep living, I could sing along. So, after it taught me the words, I did. I sang."

4. Thomas Williamson is not the only witness to go on record about the Dead-Dead Monster's apparent granting of grace.

In a 2017 interview with Clarisville Times reporter Jennifer Hatton, famed cryptozoologist and Dead-Dead Monster specialist Alfred Moulton, Ph.D. said hundreds of documents from the 19th, 20th, and current centuries indicate similar reports of Alabama residents, all of whom were involved in some kind of historic, statewide tragedy, being kindly saved from the brink of death by a "rotten-venison stinking" and "hideous" cryptid, with the unexpected "voice of an angel."

5. Another recorded case involves that of then forty-four-year-old Louise Cole. In 1918, Cole was traveling aboard a train to Montgomery when it derailed. Although dozens perished, Cole was one of the few survivors. She claimed, in a written testimony, the Dead-Dead Monster appeared to her in the train's fiery wreckage. She further explained, "When the Monster asked me if I wanted to live, I couldn't refuse. It taught me a song that kind of frightened me right there in the heavy clouds of smoke. But I sang it. And I sang it loud. There is no doubting who saved my life." Dr. Moulton argues the fact that multiple claims of similar experiences substantiate the Dead-Dead Monster's goodness. "It's **irrefutable**," Dr. Moulton says. "What we have on our hands should more fittingly be named the Dead-Dead Saint."

6. For those Alabama residents who fear death, which according to the Alabama Center of Statistical Surveys is 98.8% of the state's population, the folklore surrounding the Dead-Dead Monster provides hope that a wolf-like healer is out there, waiting to save a lucky few with a beautiful song.

Questions

1. **Which of the following best explains the purpose of paragraph 1 in the above article?**
   - ○ ~~To scare readers~~
   - ○ ~~To give necessary background information about the Dead-Dead Monster~~
   - ○ ~~To create irony~~
   - ○ ~~To support the central thesis~~

   THERE

2. **The prefix "bi" comes from Latin, meaning "two." Based on the context above, what is the meaning of the word "bipedal," as used in paragraph 1?**
   - ○ ~~Standing on two feet~~
   - ○ ~~Riding on two bicycles~~
   - ○ ~~Consisting of two halves~~
   - ○ ~~Having two sicknesses~~

   IS

3. **The author of the previous article includes statistics and research. What is the best reason for including these types of items?**
   - ○ ~~To show how fun writing can be~~
   - ○ ~~To provide support to the article's purpose~~
   - ○ ~~To trick readers into thinking the article is mainly about math~~
   - ○ ~~To impress readers with so many reliable facts~~

   ABSOLUTELY

4. In addition to releasing the statistic in the previous informational essay that 98.8% of Alabama residents fear death, the Alabama Center of Statistical Surveys provided the following charts. Please carefully read and examine the following information, and then answer the question below:

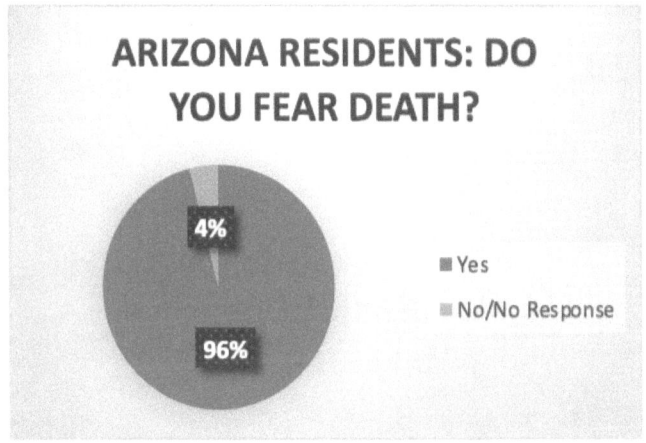

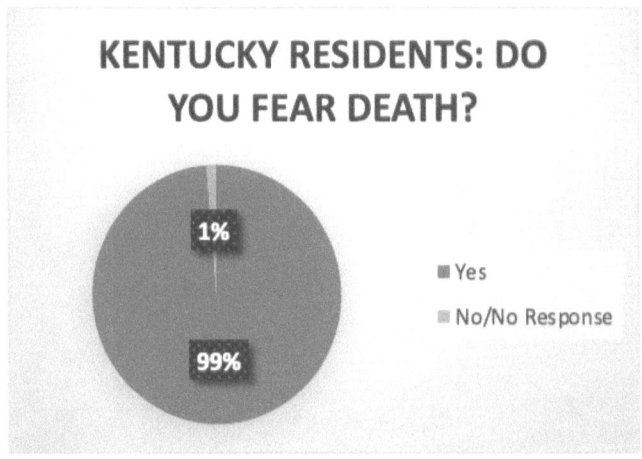

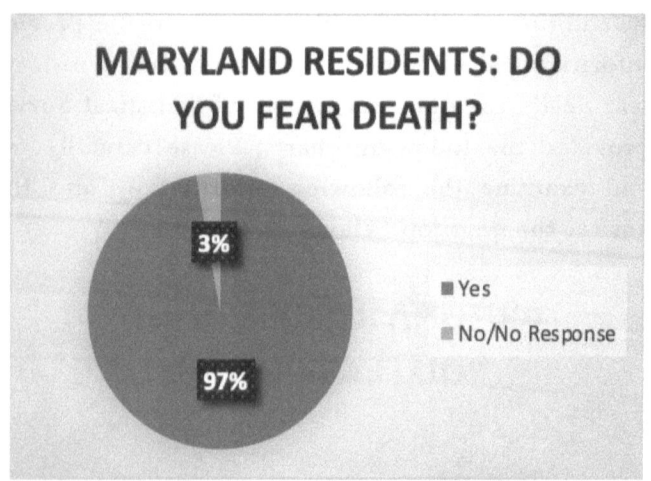

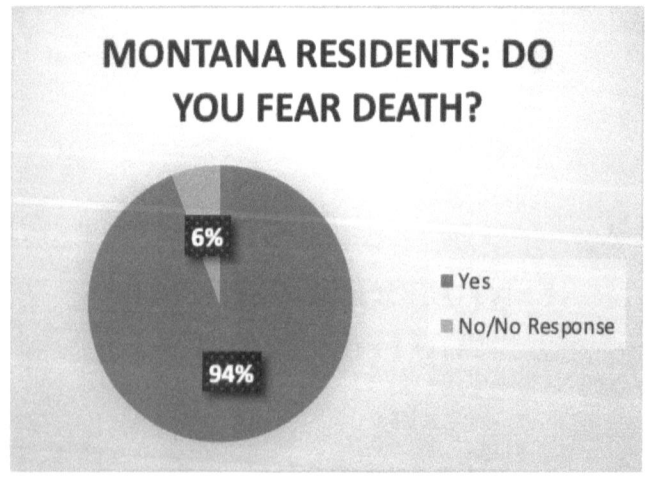

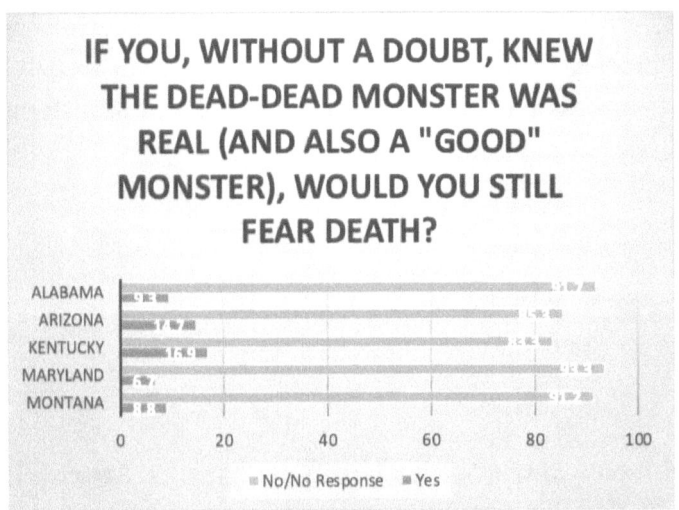

IF YOU, WITHOUT A DOUBT, KNEW
THE DEAD-DEAD MONSTER WAS
REAL (AND ALSO A "GOOD"
MONSTER), WOULD YOU STILL
FEAR DEATH?

What can best be concluded based on the information provided by the Alabama Center of Statistical Surveys?

○ ~~People living in the Northeast fear death much more than anywhere else in the country~~

○ ~~People living in the South fear death much more than anywhere else in the country~~

○ ~~No matter where people live, it is rare to fear death~~

○ ~~No matter where people live, proving the existence (and goodness) of the Dead-Dead Monster would substantially ease the fear of death~~

NO

5. **Which paragraph best serves as a transition from providing necessary background information to delving into the true mystery of the Dead-Dead Monster and its alleged goodness?**

   ○ ~~Paragraph 1~~

   ○ ~~Paragraph 2~~

   ○ ~~Paragraph 6~~

   ○ ~~All of the above~~

   SUCH

6. **The word "vile" appears in paragraph 1. After revisiting the term above and understanding its meaning based on context clues, please choose the analogy that best matches the provided example: Vile : Disgusting.**

   ○ ~~Salty : Sweet~~

   ○ ~~Burnt : Metal~~

   ○ ~~Foul : Unpleasant~~

   ○ ~~Savory : Soggy~~

   THING

7. **The article features an interview from a boy named Thomas Williamson. Williamson, in a dated interview, claimed the following: "I'm very lucky to have met the Dead-Dead Monster." Why might he have felt lucky?**

   ○ ~~Because 119 residents of his community died of cholera~~

   ○ ~~Because he got to smell the Dead-Dead Monster~~

○ Because he was able to learn a new song

○ Because the Dead-Dead Monster saved his life

AS

8. In paragraph 5, the author of the passage mentions famous cryptozoologist Dr. Alfred Moulton. Why might the author have included an interview with him?

○ To prove that the Dead-Dead Monster is real

○ To add intrigue for monster enthusiasts

○ To intimidate Sasquatch scholars

○ To enhance credibility to the central argument

A

9. Based on context clues, the definition of the word "irrefutable," which appears in paragraph 5, should be clear. Which of the following is the best antonym for the term?

○ Undeniable

○ Unquestionable

○ Disputable

○ Unassailable

GOOD

10. The Alabama Center of Statistical Surveys told 1,200 people, ranging from the ages of 12 to 96, the same information regarding the Dead-Dead Monster you

have just read. Afterward, they were asked to choose one word they feel best describes the Monster. After carefully examining the results, please answer the question that follows:

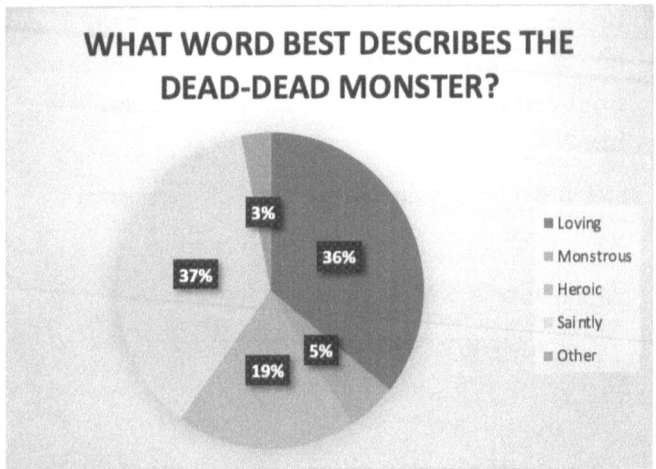

Which statement best describes how those surveyed view the Dead-Dead Monster?

- ○ ~~The vast majority of people deeply fear the Monster~~
- ○ ~~No one admires the Monster~~
- ○ ~~A slim majority of people feel terror when thinking of the Monster~~
- ○ ~~A slim majority of people feel hope when thinking of the Monster~~

MONSTER!!!

Writing Prompt

Directions: You have just read Liz Cornelius' article "A Good Monster is NOT Hard to Find," which points to possible evidence that the Dead-Dead Monster is a life-saving monster. Now, you will write an argumentative essay in which you will decide if the Dead-Dead Monster is, in your opinion, actually a monster at all.

Be specific in your writing, and be sure to use textual evidence from the original article.

Your response should be multiple paragraphs, and it should be written on the following page(s) inside this testing document.

You should do any prewriting on the provided scrap sheets of paper.

Once finished, please close your testing booklet and stay quiet until all items are collected.

I wasn't going to do this part either, but I need to say what I just read is some serious CRAP!

First of all, do you really think some wolf-looking creep that looks and smells straight up nasty is good? What about its "hauntingly red, glowing eyes"? And don't even get me started on it wearing a top hat. Are you kidding me?

Anything that wears one of those is freaky. This Dead-Dead MONSTER is from hell, and yes, it is a "monster."

Real talk, what makes a monster a monster is that it plays on fear. It thrives on fear. It relies on lies and deception and trickery and all of those other words that mean pretty much the same thing. Watch a horror movie and tell me I'm wrong. This disgusting MONSTER plays on all of this. For example, if I wanted to save some people from the grim reaper, I would save them. I wouldn't make them sing some "rather queer" song that "kind of" freaks them out. That's weird. And let me tell you more about this little song.

My great-grandfather was in a factory explosion. I don't remember which one, but it was a long time ago in some rundown city close to the beach. Who cares? Anyhow, after the fire, he started singing a new song to my grandfather when he was like five, and then my grandfather would sing it to my mom when she was coming up, and my mom sang it to me until I started having...NIGHTMARES. The song is catchy. I buy the "lullaby" comparison.

Do you want to know the lyrics? I guess
not since they aren't mentioned in Ms. Liz's
ignorant little article, but I'm going to tell you
anyway. Here goes:

"I'll go with you

Into the flames

Take me there

But not today

I'll go with you

Into the flames

Take me there

But not today

I pledge my soul to you

I do

I do

Upon that later

Dying day

Hooray, hooray."

Obviously, my great-grandfather didn't die in

the explosion, but it turns out he nearly got himself killed. He would've died if, you guessed it, THE DEAD-DEAD MONSTER wouldn't have arrived in the smoke and tricked my great-grandfather into selling his soul so he could live a few decades longer.

Until we pointed out what the lyrics actually said on his deathbed, when he started humming the song's tune, the poor, condemned man didn't realize what he'd done. Imagine how he felt then. I won't go into much detail because it isn't really your business, but I'll tell you that he was yelling for a lot of ice cubes and fire extinguishers. Yeah, not a pretty picture.

I'm sure these Thomas and Louise people realized their own upcoming eternities, too, probably as they were heading straight into those forever-unextinguishable flames hand in hand with a certain stinky, mangy MONSTER.

In conclusion, if I haven't already made it clear enough, undoubtedly, the Dead-Dead Monster is a MONSTER. Duh. Absolutely. And I know I said earlier there is no such thing as a good monster, but I've changed my mind. There is

ONE way this particular monster could be sort of "good." That would be if someone brave enough to face death head on would sacrifice those few extra offered years and just slit its deceitful, scrawny throat. Dead-Dead indeed.

—Nancy R. Melson

You have reached the end of <u>SECTION 1</u>.

Results:

Percentage: Bottom 5%

Grouping/Performance: Significantly Below Grade-Level Expectations

THAT WINTER AGO

On his fourth birthday, James prayed for snow. He did so on the first Sunday of the month, the one when the gathered believers, who were to celebrate birthdays in the coming thirty-one days of January, paraded to the altar to receive the blessing of the birthday song, sung by the Cedarsville United Methodist Church's overly ambitious choir. While everyone waited on ninety-nine-year-old Estelle Hardy to shuffle to the front, James jumped up the single stair that separated him from the understood spotlight and stole the podium from Reverend Nelson, the chap-cheeked boy's grandfather, and he led a prayer, *the* prayer. The little boy closed his eyes and spoke with so much force—*belief*—into the microphone that even the easily amused teenagers in those crowded, mouse-gnawed pews in the back knew to hush up and mouth "amen." James had never seen snow. None of them had, but according to the weather reporter on the radio, there was actually a chance.

When it blanketed the town that night, James knew he was the reason why.

On his fifth birthday, James prayed for snow. Not because he wanted to experience the joy of making a snow angel again or to reignite the struggle of constructing a snowman. It wasn't because he craved another bowl of sugary snow cream either. Or because he wanted to see how another snowball fight might end. He prayed because he wanted all those people to come back—the ones who'd been out with him among it all and vanished. His parents. His grandparents. Ms. Hardy. Even snaggle-toothed Ralph Nash, the neighbor kid who used to sit alone in his yard on Sunday mornings and slurp worms from the damp soil. He thought if the wintery sky opened again, it might be to allow the lost—everyone he'd ever known—to return.

When nothing came, James closed his eyes and tried again.

On his eleventh birthday, James prayed for snow. Just as he had every day for the past seven years. Of course, he prayed for it in winter, sitting at his family's old kitchen table, with his mother's soup-stained quilt draped over his back, trapping his dense clouds of breath. With the silent company of his stained and balding stuffed dinosaurs and dogs. But he even prayed for snow in the summer as he scavenged, coated with mud and sweat, as far as he could see, for dandelions and clovers. And, too, as he stood under the plum trees and waited for the fruit to drop because he still could not reach the bent limbs. He prayed as he went from lonely house to lonely house, searching cabinets for beans and soups. Stale chips, crackers, and cookies. Searching freezers for strawberries and cherries. Popsicles and pies.

When the sky stayed clear, he didn't give up.

On his eighteenth birthday, James prayed for snow. So that, with its return, he might have someone to touch. A hand to hold. Lips to kiss. He prayed to hear a voice that might speak his name. And for a body to sit outdoors, against his own, on a humid evening to watch the lightning bugs flicker. A body that could keep him company as he fell off, perhaps under a full moon, into his dreams.

When the clouds proved to be empty, James bowed his head and asked again.

On his twenty-first birthday, James prayed for snow. He prayed for snow so he might pull the books off his parents' dusty shelves and be reminded of the sounds the letters made. What the words meant. To be reminded that stories could have happy endings.

When the skies failed him, he didn't stop.

On his twenty-ninth birthday, James prayed for snow. He prayed for snow so that, with it, he might have a son of his own. A daughter. A wife. A career. A reason to laugh. To celebrate. Shout. Even, he prayed, another reason for him to cry.

When nothing came from above, he kept at it.

On his thirty-eighth birthday, James prayed for snow. For it to come. For it to please, please come. Not even for it only to bring them back, but for it, this time, if it could, to just come and to not spare him. To take him. To take him far away. Away with the others. Please. Please, with the others. Please, please. He prayed for snow, too, on his forty-second birthday and his fifty-sixth. His fifty-ninth and sixty-third. He kept at it, more determined by each passing day. Month. Year. On his sixty-seventh birthday. His seventy-first. Seventy-second. Seventy-third. Fourth and fifth.

When the moon and stars shone brightly in the clear sky, he still bowed his head.

On his eighty-fourth birthday, James prayed for snow. When the white shadows of falling flakes decorated his bedroom wall, he didn't bother going to his window to make sure his eyes weren't playing a trick on him; instead, he, with his father's too-big, ragged clothes and dirty, cut skin, and teeth that no longer sat right in his gums, stayed put, with his covered legs spilling out of the only bed he'd ever known. Listening for those voices. For the doorknob to turn. Waiting for those familiar shadows to darken his bedroom's doorframe. For those he loved to wrap their arms around him once again. Praying. Always, always praying.

When snow blanketed the town that night, James prayed he was the reason why.

THERE GOES THEM
GHOST CHILDREN

Dear Bonnie,

I'm writing to ask for your forgiveness. The truth is that I haven't ever stopped thinking about you. How I failed you. What I let happen to you.

I've known what I've needed to do for a long time to get my words to you, but I've just now gotten the courage to do it. Now that your mama's gone and it's just me drowning in all this loneliness. All this guilt.

I hope this all isn't for nothing.

Maybe it's crazy. Maybe it's more than crazy. But I need you to know my side of what happened that night.

Please read this letter, Bon. Please.

You have to understand, when you refused to get out of the car after we pulled under that shiny new carport frame that connected to this here house and property we'd gotten such a good deal on, I thought you were mad at me and your mama for uprooting you from your friends.

We couldn't believe you were acting the way you were for anything other than you not wanting to let them girls go.

When you told us it was because you were seeing mean little ghost children in the windows and running around the trees, we sure didn't believe you.

Who would've?

We didn't see a thing. Hear nothing either. Not so much as a shadow or a whisper.

You probably remember us all sitting there for the longest time in the station wagon, me and your mama trying to convince you to get out and come inside the house with us. How you wouldn't help us unload the trailer we'd barely managed to get hitched up. How you wouldn't even undo your seatbelt. How you were just yelling, terrified of sorts. "I ain't getting close to them ghost children! I ain't getting close to them ghost children!"

It was the biggest mess of nonsense me and your mama'd heard in our lives.

We watched you as you wrestled yourself deep into your vinyl seat, hugging that little stuffed bear you had so tight against you, like it was your own soul that you were pushing back in your body.

I didn't ever tell your mama this, but I see you that same way, all scared like, cowering and big-eyed, when I close my eyes for sleep that rarely comes.

I have since that night, Bon.

The truth is, me and your mama had never much seen you act that way. Like a silly, foolish child is what we thought.

We didn't know what to do with you, so when we told you to just keep on while we took the boxes inside, we thought that was fine enough.

We thought you'd cave in and help us.

I think we both hoped so.

But you didn't, of course.

I know you have to remember, but you just sat out there crying and fussing.

We were done so plumb flustered by the time we'd gotten everything inside by ourselves that we thought we'd just let you sit out there and stew long into the night.

We were wrong, Bon, for thinking such a thing, especially with your mind full of spirits. We were so wrong.

Please forgive me. Please, darling.

We watched you when we were inside. Your mama peeked through the bedroom blinds and got a good look at you after we tore open that first box full of broken plates. Seeing them plates like that made her remember what being really frustrated was.

I remember her putting that box down and sitting on the floor. She was talking real soft, saying something about how you were probably acting like you were because you were sad.

That made us both feel kind of sorry for you, but it isn't easy to apologize once you're set in your ways. Even when those ways are wrong. Maybe especially when those ways are wrong.

Do you know your mama was watching you most of the evening?

Every ten minutes or so, she'd tell me to carry on unpacking, and she'd go to the back bedroom and look out at you, the porch lights catching you at just the right angle.

She'd come back and give me a full report.

Same thing each time, too. You with your tear-streaked face, carrying on like something wild.

She told me we should go out there and get you. She told me that.

I ain't proud of what I did, but I told her no.

It's my fault, Bon. I'm sorry to say it, but it is my fault.

I told her we'd wait until the boxes on the counter by the stove were unpacked. Then we'd do it. "We'll go out there together," I said. "Give her just a little more time to pout around. She'll sleep better because of it."

I can hear myself saying those exact words.

I said it all joke-like. Even did a little chuckle at the end. I can still hear that stupid sound I made, too.

If only I'd listened to your mama.

And your mama, she just shrugged her shoulders and carried on.

Wasn't no point in arguing with me. She knew as much.

You have to understand, I hadn't ever seen any spirits. I didn't believe in those kinds of things. I didn't know anybody else who did either.

What you were spouting just wasn't possible to me.

That's why I didn't believe you. I know I should've, but I just didn't. That's why, Bon.

Forgive me.

When your mama got busy with unwrapping all the paper towels we'd put around her teapots, I told her to keep on. I told her I'd go take a look at you.

After all them times your mama'd come back and reported you were fine, I believed my eyes were just tricking me. I remember blinking them a dozen times at least.

No matter what I did, it wasn't helping.

I could see the light on in that old station wagon. Wasn't no questioning that. But the door was open, and your seat was empty except for your bear.

As bad as I wanted to be wrong, I knew. I could feel in my insides that something wasn't right. Until that moment, I hadn't thought a thing in the world about you sitting out there in that car. I swear it. But when I saw that door swung back, I felt my stomach sink to my knees.

I came around that bedroom door and took off down the hall. Shouting. Yelling. Whatever you want to call it, I was doing it.

Your mama didn't have to ask me what was going on.

Somehow, she knew.

She dropped one of her teapots and took off after me out the door.

Both of us barefooted.

We were yelling something awful.

Carol and Tim, those were our neighbors at the time, they turned on their own porch lights and came out and helped us look for you. Those people just had to ask your name once, and they knew it as good as their own. Carol had her hair in rollers and was wearing her housecoat. Tim was in nothing but his boxer shorts. They didn't seem to think a thing about how they looked to us either. They were out there calling just as loud as me and your mama. Maybe louder, thinking back on it.

We were all looking for you. Carol told us to keep on, and she'd call the neighborhood watch. She did, too, and they came. Fast. Panicky. Seemed that way at least, even then in that moment. About the whole neighborhood. Forty folks or so. Half-dressed and all kinds of ugly.

We were looking, Bon. All of us.

Those folks didn't know us from Adam, but they kept asking to see your picture.

I undid my wallet and showed them the one you'd had taken in school the year before. I tried to turn that image of you toward the light whenever anybody asked.

Wasn't probably going to be any other little girl just roaming around by herself in the dark, but I showed them. Every time, I showed them.

We looked everywhere.

Honest. I swear it. On your mama's soul, I swear it.

The police showed up. Sirens blaring. Fire trucks came too.

Everybody was asking questions and looking at that photo of you. We kept on throughout the night, till after the sun had come up and was warming us the next morning.

All those folks, dirty and breathless, slowly went on home. Even the cops eventually excused themselves because they were past due for a shift change.

Carol and Tim stayed around until the last soul left, and then Tim grabbed my shoulder and gave me the biggest squeeze I'd ever felt. He stared right directly into my eyes, and I still remember his words. Won't ever forget them. He said, "I should have told you the place was cursed when I saw you and your wife out looking to buy, but I didn't know you all had a little one." Him and Carol both looked like they were about to cry when he said it. He wasn't finished, though. I could tell it by the way he'd cut himself off. He took a deep breath—a real big one, Bon—and then he went on. "Hurts my heart to say as much, but your girl ain't coming back."

You know it isn't in my nature for me not to have anything to say, but I was speechless.

Honestly, neither one of us said a word. We couldn't, Bon. We just turned and went back on with our searching.

I know this doesn't make up for what happened, but do you know that while your mama was still alive and able that we didn't stop? She'd spend all day out. Looking everywhere. Researching missing kids from the years before. At the dinky little library. Reading old books. Trying, and failing, to make contact with their families. Making trips across the county. Getting hung up on and doors slammed in her face. When I'd get home from my shift at Sammy's Auto, she'd be ready for us to head out before I had the time to wash off good. Before I'd even had a bite of dinner. There was always, according to her, another rock to overturn.

I believe it's that searching that kept us together, too. I know she had to blame me, but the hope that we might find you must've been stronger than that anger.

We went to every river, ditch, and patch of woods for miles. For miles, and we didn't uncover a thing. There was no trace of you at all except that toy bear just sitting there as pretty as it pleased in your seat in the car.

We hated everybody in this neighborhood. This whole town, really. We did. All of them. Even after they came out that night, we couldn't help but hate them. After it first happened and they insisted on leaving us casseroles on our porch, we let the ants eat them. If only we would've known, Bon. If only they would've told us.

We didn't ever leave because, for the longest time, we kept hope going that you might come back.

As crazy as it sounds, that's the truth.

I prayed day and night that you would return to us.

I even prayed that those ghost children you saw might come back, too. That I could see them. Just once. Just once, Bon, so I'd know for myself that they were real. To see for myself that they could've taken you.

A couple of months before your mama passed, she was dreaming more and more. I'd stay awake and listen to her. She'd say, "There goes them ghost children! There goes them ghost children! There goes them ghost children!" Just repeating those words for hours upon hours.

Even then, she was trying to find you. I know she was.

Truth is, now that your mama's gone, I'm tired. Of searching. Of holding onto this guilt.

I can't take it no more either.

I know I won't see you again. It's been hard for me to accept, but I know it's the truth.

I'm leaving this property for good, leaving this whole place behind.

Finally decided it.

Already sold it to a nice couple. They have two kids. A boy and girl. Wild little things. Maybe I should have told them about you. About what happened to you. About how it had to have been the ghost children. But I ain't.

And I won't.

I can't, Bon. I'm sorry for it, but I can't.

Maybe that silence makes me just like everybody else in this Godforsaken place. I can't argue with that.

But I need you to read this letter. More than anything, I just need you to know how sorry I am.

If it's true and you're with them now, which I have to believe you are, you'll come back. Leaving these words is the only way I know how to reach you.

You have to understand how sorry I am. For all of it, Bon. For all of it, I'm sorry.

I ask that you forgive me. For what I let happen to you. For the two other kids I didn't protect. For all of it.

Please.

Sincerely,
Your father

P. S. If you're a member of the Donaldson family and are reading this letter, I'm sorry for what's happened to your children. I ask your forgiveness much the same.

CROCODILE TEARS DIDN'T CAUSE THE FLOOD

Once upon a time, long after they'd left their families and friends and jobs and had moved to the top of the hill so very, very far away, the man and woman went outside under the comfortable silence of the stars and knelt on the cool, worm moist dirt. There, they held one another. And they asked.

Begged.

Prayed.

They wept together, hoping for their dreamed miracle to *finally* come.

After a few hours, a flock of overhead rain crows interrupted them, announcing it was time to go inside. The pair raised their heads and kissed, falling into one another as they opened the door.

At midnight, an unusually rowdy *thump thumping* crashed above them on their cedar-shingled roof. The husband and wife rose from their just-warm pillows and switched on their lamps, suspecting—*believing*—the cause was neither rain nor hail.

They looked to one another, and, although they tried to contain themselves, they couldn't. They smiled.

The man grabbed the woman's hand, and, together, they approached the bedroom's lone window. It was then that they saw the moon-lit robots that fell from the sky.

The couple had not imagined their child as possessing wiring instead of veins—or cold, empty space rather than blood—but they didn't mind.

They were happy—so very happy that they didn't think to complain either that the bodies did not fall in whole.

The man and woman trembled laughing as shimmering index fingers lodged in the swaying oak branches and as iron ankles smushed the many multiplying mushrooms. They howled, especially joyously, as a metallic head crashed into the very glass that separated them from the lavish storm.

Sarah.

Samuel.

Ivey.

Ian.

They dreamed of the names the innocent face might soon receive. From the new parents. From *them*.

Still holding the other, the married pair ran to get their torn-off clothes, which remained in their bedside piles. They threw them back on, lopsided and with skipped buttons.

He retrieved the rubber boots, and she darted for the rain jackets. Both were so lost in the moment that neither of them realized the things they held in their hands would be of no use in the kind of flood that poured upon their hill.

Dressed, they went onto the porch and stood covered from the splendid wreckage. Shouting. Celebrating, still.

The storm raged until daybreak and ended with one final downpour of hazel and amber eyeballs. Although many of them rolled into the overgrown flowerbeds and got stuck in torn cobwebs that still stretched from the porch's mildewed columns, the new mother and father grabbed what they could, not even taking the time to make sure they had matching pairs.

They waded through the awaiting parts. All the way out until they were in the center of it all.

There, they prayed again, offering thanks. For the perfect child, somewhere among the sparkling, dented, beautiful mess, that awaited them.

For their happy ever after.

Versions of these stories first appeared
in the following publications:

"Raising Again" in *Short Beasts*

"The Guide to King George" in *BULL*

"Our Patches" in *The Dead Mule*

"To Take, To Leave" in *Psychopomp*

"Festival of Kites" in *Reflex Press*

"The Browne Transcript" in *Drunk Monkeys*

"Claire & Hank" in *Necessary Fiction*

"Do You Remember?" in *Ghost Parachute*

"Remembrance Day" in *Vending Machine Press*

"Peaches' Menagerie" in *Signal Mountain Review*

"From 1973" (originally appeared as "Eli's Ghost") in *Five:2:One*

"Nancy R. Melson's State ELA Exam, Section 1: The Dead-Dead Monster" in *Superstition Review*

"That Winter Ago" in *The Argonaut*

"There Goes Them Ghost Children" in *Signal Mountain Review*

"Crocodile Tears Didn't Cause the Flood" in *Bear Creek Gazette*

ACKNOWLEDGEMENTS

This book would not have been possible without the unwavering support of my family. To Meredith, Mollie, June, and Kirby, I love you. Thank you for everything.

Thank you to all those fantastic folks back home in Alabama and in Tennessee. Family. Friends. You know who you are.

Also, thank you to Kelly Ian (at *Short Beasts*), Ben Drevlow (at *BULL*), Valerie MacEwan (at *The Dead Mule*), Sequoia Nagamatsu (at *Psychopomp*), Judy Darley (at *Reflex Press*), Kolleen Carney Hoepfner (at *Drunk Monkeys*), Lacey N. Dunham (at *Necessary Fiction*), Brett Pribble (at *Ghost Parachute*), Michael Lafontaine (at *Vending Machine Press*), Sarah Einstein and Keily Blair (at *Signal Mountain Review*), Nathan Schwartz (at *Five:2:One*), Trish C. Murphy (at *Superstition Review*), Sheldon Lee Compton (at *The Argonaut*), and Stuart Buck (at *Bear Creek Gazette*) for publishing versions of these stories. It's an honor to have my words included in your magazines.

Thank you to all of the wonderful people who helped get this book ready and out. Charlie and Lindsay, I'll always be grateful for you giving this book a publishing home—and for your recommendations on how to take it to the next level. Peter, thank you for the perfect cover. Lori, thank you for being the best publicist around. You have helped me accomplish some seemingly impossible dreams.

Many of these stories were produced during my MFA years at Queens. I must extend my sincere gratitude to all the wonderful writers I was able to work alongside in my small group workshops, including Kim, Allison, Ash, Timothy, and many, many others. Thank you as well to the professors who shaped so much of my time in the program. Specifically, thank you to Elissa Schappell for helping me better understand my vision, motivating me to keep going, and pushing me to make my stories be the best they could be. Thank you to Fred Leebron for always offering such gracious support. Thank you to Patricia Powell for the sincere kindness and encouragement you extended to me and everyone in our small group.

Thank you to all of those teachers who've shaped me throughout the years. Not just at Queens, but from elementary school and onward.

I must give an immense thank you to my students—the former and the current. You inspire me, and I'm grateful for the sincere gift I've had in this life of being able to share words and stories with you.

Finally, thank you, dear reader. There would be no place for written stories without you.

BIO

 **B**radley Sides is the author of two short story collections, *Those Fantastic Lives* and *Crocodile Tears Didn't Cause the Flood*. His writing appears in *Chicago Review of Books*, *Electric Literature*, *Los Angeles Review of Books*, *The Millions*, *The Rumpus*, and elsewhere. His fiction has been nominated for Year's Best Weird Fiction and featured on *LeVar Burton Reads*. He holds an MFA from Queens University of Charlotte, where he served as Fiction Editor of *Qu*. Currently, he lives in Huntsville, Alabama, with his wife. On most days, he can be found teaching writing at Calhoun Community College. For more, visit bradley-sides.com.